A Love Lost in Positano

A Love Lost in Positano

D.P. Rosano

"Positano is a dream place that isn't quite real when you are there
and becomes beckoningly real after you have gone."
– John Steinbeck

To Linda and Kristen

May 17, 2007

Sometimes I think that all I have of Gaia is the dream.

My mind is suspended partway between sleep and wakefulness, a contented smile lingering on my lips, eyelashes fluttering lightly as my conscious self begins to dawn.

Then my eyes flash open, the smile disappears in pain, and a pile of imagined letters flutter before me.

* * * *

Three years ago, I was immersed in the war that had drained most of my energy and, it seemed, all of my emotion. I was stationed in Afghanistan, in the Kabul office of the State Department, and spent long hours translating clipped recordings of conversation from Pashto and Farsi, languages I had studied while at the university but only mastered once my life and life's work depended on it.

From scratchy audio files to shards of handwritten notes, my work combined the monotonous exercise of an archeologist dusting off an ancient stone with the keen awareness that a missed word or nuance could get someone killed. I knew that guessing right might put a wanted man in the crosshairs of an American drone, but guessing wrong could annihilate an innocent family instead.

Spending long days briefing my civilian leaders, who briefed their military counterparts, in the subtleties of culture and tradition of the locals, was tiring and exhilarating, all at the same time. I knew I was expected to have the talents of both a linguist and a cultural attaché, to be mindful of Afghanistan's civilian and government traditions, and careful not to step on the toes of the indigenous military powers. It was a tricky balancing act, to say the least.

Spending month after month worrying about other people's egos – both American and Afghan – left little time to worry about my own ego. I needed a break. Rotating back to the States was still a ways off so a quick R&R in Italy seemed like the best way to re-balance my life.

After eighteen months on station, short periods of rest were not hard to get approved, so I took a week off and headed for Positano, on Italy's Amalfi Coast. I had heard and read about the little fishing village turned Europhile getaway, and it seemed like the perfect prescription for what ailed me.

I stuffed my rucksack with clean clothes then reached for my laptop and satellite phone. I hefted the computer, looked at it with resignation, then slid it back into the desk drawer, pleased that I had cut the cord that bound me to it. I was not so successful with the sat-phone, knowing that I couldn't be out of touch with the station completely.

A driver handling a dusty station truck took me to the Hamid Karzai International Airport on the edge of Kabul, where I transferred to a military hop out of country. Another stop and another plane, and I landed in Rome aboard a commercial flight dropping into Leonardo da Vinci Airport. I gave half a thought to spending a night there, but the din of activity reminded me of what I was trying to get away from. Instead, I boarded an Italian train to Sorrento, where I transferred once again, this time to a small, un-air-conditioned taxi for the drive to Positano.

As the car left Sorrento, the countryside smoothed out and the long strip of blacktop in front of me provided time to unwind and begin to reset my inner engine to a slower speed. Not long afterward, the cabbie embarked on a narrow winding strip of road that hugged the ridge of mountain that rose to unseen heights on my left just as the mountain fell into the sea immediately to my right. It was not exactly mountain goat territory, but I did occasionally wish that the driver would slow down and prevent the tires from screeching their way around the dead man's curves.

We were on the Viale Pasitea when, suddenly, the car came to a stop and the driver hopped out to retrieve my rucksack from the trunk. On my left was a long line of single story shops and cafés; on my right a sheer drop into the Mediterranean Sea. I couldn't see the hotel that was my destination, so I asked the driver.

"Dov'é la Casa Albertina?"

The driver pointed to a narrow opening between two of the shops, and I saw a set of stone steps inclining upward and off into the slope of the hillside.

I retrieved my bag and ducked between the shops and started the climb to the hotel. It was a bit of a struggle but, when I reached the summit and looked back over my shoulder I was blown away by the scene that draped before me. The Mediterranean Sea sparkled below and for infinite miles to the horizon. The azure sky above and the multi-colored roofs of the buildings beside and below me were ample proof that I had chosen the right place for my R&R.

After checking in with the smiling desk clerk, I retired to my room. Tossing my bag on the bed and throwing the drapes open I took in the scene that would be mine for the next five days. Every room in Casa Albertina had a private balcony with several chairs and a small table. I pulled on the handles of the huge windowed doors and stepped out into what seemed like a Mediterranean fantasy. The balcony looked down on the beach hundreds of feet below, and on the town which surrounded the green and gold dome of the local church, the Chiesa di Santa Maria Assunta.

It was a breathtaking introduction to life in Positano and, for a moment, I couldn't believe I was actually here. It was far more captivating than even the most romantic descriptions had prepared me for. I leaned on the low stone wall that encircled my balcony, wanting to memorize the scene and make it a part of my whole being, something that I could take back with me to Kabul.

The thought of the war, the State Department work, and Kabul itself invaded my thoughts for only a moment, then I shifted back to Positano, confirming my plan to be here, not there – at least for this short time.

I enjoyed a simple dinner on the terrace of the hotel's restaurant. With its access to the sea, my first meal had to be some sort of fish. After querying the waiter as to what's good – "*Tutti*" he said, with a typical Italian shrug, "everything" – I settled on a plate of thin noodles and crab meat, a specialty of the Amalfi Coast. The delicate noodles were dressed in lightly salted butter, and the crab meat was flaky and also dressed in a butter sauce. Although the serving seemed large when it arrived at my table, I surprised myself by quickly finishing it off.

Lazily settling back in the chair, I sipped at the second glass of white wine brought out by the waiter. Normally, I preferred red wine but the dish demanded something softer and fresher, so the local Fiano di Avellino was a perfect match. I relaxed a while, taking in the moments approaching sunset. With the fresh air and fresher aromas of lemon trees surrounding the hotel, I gazed out at the sun as it settled down on the sea, leaving a yellow orange blaze across the horizon.

Some wine, the scent of bougainvillea. How could I not be relaxed at that moment?

I sipped from the glass and let the cool liquid glide down my throat. Placing it down on the table, I looked up and saw that, while I was taken in by the sunset, I had failed to notice the young woman leaning on the stone railing of the terrace, facing out to sea, her back to me.

Long brown hair hung down across sun-tanned shoulders, shoulders exposed by the green, pink, and blue sundress she wore. She breathed a long sigh and leaned her head back to stare up at the sky above that was slowly dimming in the fading light. She turned around, faced my direction and, for a brief second, smiled slightly, then strode quietly across the stones to a small table by the edge of the terrazza.

A waiter appeared behind her bearing a tray with a glass of white wine, a bowl of olives, and a basket of bread. I could hear them speaking Italian, but it seemed like it wasn't her native tongue.

"*Efcharistó*" slipped from her mouth, confirming that she wasn't Italian.

But what language was that?

Her attention was drawn to the wine and olives, but mine was drawn to her. Her complexion was smooth and lightly bronzed, like the toned shoulders that held the thin straps of her dress. Her dark brown hair was simply cut and straight, but worn long, and her willowy legs stretched out beneath the table in a languid pose. Long slender fingers encircled the wine glass as she tipped it to her mouth. I could not see her eyes from my angle, but my imagination greedily filled in the details.

I felt like a voyeur, sneaking looks in her direction, but was captivated by her and couldn't resist. At one point she leaned over to straighten the buckle on her sandals, leaning in my direction, and when she sat back up she glanced in my direction again. This time, her smile lingered a second longer, enough to give me a pleasurable chill.

"*Buon giorno*," I offered in her direction, still not sure of her nationality or language.

"Hello," she responded in easy English. Possibly an American? Thoughts of "come here often" crossed my mind, but I winced at my own lack of originality.

Still, I was desperate to keep the conversation going and had no idea what to say next.

The young lady made my effort a bit easier by continuing to look in my direction, an act that also made me slightly nervous. I was never one for easy lines, and what meager skills I had in that department abandoned me now.

"It's a beautiful sky," she said. But I blushed because I was staring at her, not the sky, and maybe she was trying to get me to look away.

"Yes, amazing," I replied. Wow, my lack of creative thought was stunning.

Without enough encouragement from me, she turned her attention back to the plate of olives and bread on her table, sipping occasionally from the wine glass.

"People say Positano is the most romantic place in Italy," I blurted. Bad opening. What was I doing talking about romance?

She giggled a bit, but covered her mouth, and batted her eyes twice. It seemed like she was willing to forgive my *faux pas*, but what I really needed was a big hole to fall into.

"So I've heard," she returned, "although I've never had the opportunity to test it."

And I realized that she was throwing me a lifeline.

"My name's Danny."

"Gaia," she replied. Now I knew it; she's Greek, but her mastery of English suggests American too?

For a few moments, it seemed that conversation had stalled, and I felt once again the pressure to restore it. The seconds ticked by, seeming more like hours, and I had to face the reality that I had nothing interesting to say, at least not across the terrace.

So I decided to close the gap. Closeness would enhance conversation.

"If you're alone, may I join you?"

She didn't speak, but lifted her glass in the age-old salutation, and smiled back at me. That was enough.

I rose from my chair, stepped quickly toward her table, and took a seat across from her. Now I could see her eyes, even in the fading light. They were brown, but with a glint of green flecks in them. The subtle hint of red lipstick lit up both her eyes and her skin, and I breathed a sigh of thanks to the gods of Positano.

That all happened in 2004, that and more, and here I was again back at Positano, still infatuated with Gaia, still wondering what had become of her.

My Journal – July 14, 2004

Prompted by my sister, I bought a journal for this trip. I'm on leave from an assignment with the State Department, working in Afghanistan to improve relations with the village leaders. Sis had told me that the war theatre had hardened me – she was right – that I should go to some beautiful place, somewhere out of the war zone, maybe on the coast of Italy, and forget the war and Afghanistan. And that I should write my thoughts down in a journal. She said that I could bring the journal back to my bombed-out house in the war zone and read the entries – "repeat as necessary" she said – and the memory of them would soften me.

So I bought this journal. I had only inscribed a few paragraphs in it before reaching the terrazza at Casa Albertina, and meeting Gaia.

We talked for a long time, past sunset, and we watched as the stars flicked on in the sky above us. She was alternately funny and serious, but her words and thoughts had an amazing depth to them. I realized several times that I was so focused on her when she spoke that I forgot that the silence meant I was supposed to chime in.

"You're funny, you know," she said. "That's just what I need."

"Why's that?" It seemed too serious a comment. She told me she was a student, so I asked, "What are you studying?"

"History."

"Really. That's great. I studied history; now I work for the State Department."

Gaia offered a peremptory nod. It wasn't that she didn't like my response, just that it seemed to enter into dangerous territory. My first strikeout of the evening.

It didn't slow the conversation though, and we soon returned to talking about travel, what we thought of Italy – "It's unbelievably beautiful here" she said – and even what our plans were for the future.

"I guess I'll finish up, get my degree, maybe go on for a Masters," she said, "and teach. Yeah, I think I'll teach."

It was amusing, it seemed like Gaia was just deciding what to do with her life as we sat there under the stars over the Mediterranean Sea. I watched her eyes light up as she talked about her plans, and watched as a subtle shadow passed over her face at other moments. I considered the reasons, and thought hard about what signals she was sending that preceded each shifting mood, but then I let it pass. Part of my training as a translator was linked to my past life in military intelligence, when I applied techniques of profiling and psychology to tease out the truth from those I interviewed, and thought that now, with Gaia, maybe I was letting my old life intrude upon my new one.

I wanted to shut that life out of Positano, and did so deliberately.

After a couple hours of talking and the blaze of sunset had been replaced by the twinkle of stars in the Mediterranean firmament, the time was getting late and I feared that, if Gaia went off the bed, I'd miss my chance to see her again.

"Will you be in Positano long," I asked.

"Five days."

I too was staying five, so that was perfect. I relaxed, figuring that if I could avoid making a complete wreck of the evening I would have more time to get to know Gaia before week's end.

We continued to share thoughts about Italy and, at times, open up about our lives. I could tell her some information, like my education and early career in the State Department. I couldn't tell her much about my service in Afghanistan – such commentary seemed to close her up – and I couldn't open up much about my time as a profiler and interrogation specialist for the American military. The psychological techniques I used then were unique to the small unit I was a part of, techniques that depended almost solely on recognizing facial tics and changes in skin temperature to differentiate between truth and falsehood. What we did, and what we found out in those closed sessions with suspects, could never be made public.

Just before midnight, she reached up to cover her mouth as a tired yawn escaped.

"I think I better get some sleep."

"Unless you have plans for tomorrow, can I see you then?"

"Sure," she said quickly.

We walked inside and down separate hallways of Casa Albertina to our rooms. So, here I am writing notes in this journal. They are not the entries that I had thought I'd be writing, about peace and serenity on the Amalfi Coast, but here they are.

Maybe this is the most beautiful place in Italy.

May 17, 2007

"Signor d'Amato," the desk clerk said to me as I returned from the terrazza. He was not on duty when I checked in that afternoon and he smiled broadly when he recognized me.

"It's so good to see you. How have you been?"

I just nodded without a spoken reply.

His smile faded, though just for a fraction of a second, before returning to his face with a bit of effort.

"Si, Umberto, I'm back," I said. It was a joyless response.

"It's been, what, a year?" he continued.

"*Si.*"

The frown returned to Umberto, and held there.

"Still looking?" he asked.

I stared back at him, but said nothing. I confronted this question in my mind on a daily basis, but when someone else asked the same thing, it was hard for me to know how to reply.

Umberto fidgeted, shifting from one foot to the other, as we both considered what to say next.

"It's warm today," he offered weakly. "The beach is warm. I think you would like a few hours by the water."

He sounded like a therapist trying to find a solution for my momentary comfort.

I stared blankly at the floor, then slowly nodded, chin slightly bobbing to indicate my acceptance of Umberto's suggestion. It was true I could use some down time, maybe under the warming rays of the sun on Positano's stony beach. As long as I could set aside my thoughts and close my eyes for a while.

As I turned to leave, I could see that Umberto raised his chin, sighed slightly, and stared at me as I exited the lobby.

My Journal – July 15, 2004

Morning came early for me, prompted by the excitement of seeing Gaia again.

Trying to be patient and prepare myself properly, I showered, shaved, and dressed in the best shirt I had in my rucksack. It was still a bit rumpled, so I pulled it off and searched for an iron in the room. Finding the tool, I plugged it in but had to wait a painful ten minutes for it to warm up. Finally, impatiently, I applied the tepid iron to the shirt and managed to press out the worst wrinkles.

"It'll have to do," I said to myself while holding the shirt at arm's length.

Casa Albertina serves a very fine *prima colazione*, the first meal of the day, and doesn't rest solely on the European tradition of coffee and rolls. There were several types of sliced meat, mountains of cheeses, fresh rolls and aromatic bread, and coffee, espresso, and cappuccino for the guests.

When I arrived in the breakfast room, there was a middle-aged couple tending to their plates of food without speaking. The looked like they had already shared many meals, both at home and away, over years of marriage. Their easy companionship made it clear that it wasn't that they were tired of each other's company; they probably had just already said most everything that had to be said.

Across the way, I saw two young women, likely of British origin given their accented conversation, talking with animated whispers about the sites they intended to take in that day. One was set on going straight to Pompeii, the other worried that the tour of the ancient city would absorb all their time and there would be no time to hike the trails above Positano and Amalfi. With no end in sight for their debate, I turned my attention to the rest of the dining room.

A forty-something woman in what clearly seemed to be American clothes sat with her young daughter and even younger son. They ate mostly in quiet, but the little boy was more intent on playing with his roll than eating it, and his mother was more intent on giving him lessons in proper behavior than consuming her own breakfast.

I chose my food, sat down at a table near the outside terrazza, and faced the door so that I wouldn't miss the entry of anyone – well, someone in particular.

It was two rounds of espresso before Gaia entered. She wore a gauzy white top tied with a string at the neck, over powder blue pants. The bright yellow strap sandals emphasized her tan.

She stopped at the door expectantly, scanned the room, then smiled in my direction when she saw me. It felt like some sort of unearned reward, but I was grateful for it. I watched as she walked in my direction, taking in her smile, her stride, and the promise of some time with her.

Settling into the chair across from me and facing the sea, Gaia smiled again, this time more broadly. She rested her chin on her right hand and said, matter of factly, "So, what should we do today?"

I couldn't hide the smile that stretched across my face, then blushed when I realized how obvious I was. But I was ready for any time with Gaia, minutes or hours, but a whole day had not yet entered my imagination.

"Well, let's see," I stammered, trying to recall some special activity that probably lurked in the pages of the unread guidebook on my nightstand. I hoped that I would quickly come up with a fascinating, one-of-a-kind daytrip to wrap us up in, but my mind was a blank.

"Why don't we just start on the beach," she said. "It's still early, and the famous black stones of Positano won't be hot yet." She leaned forward and smiled, then said, "And we can just luxuriate in the beauty of the Amalfi Coast."

Her smile had the same effect as the warm sun on my face. The green specks in her eyes twinkled, and she reached across the table to touch my hand.

"Sounds great," I replied, the thrill of it all still holding me in suspense.

"Okay, then," Gaia said quickly, and she moved into planning mode.

"Let me get some breakfast and coffee, then we'll go."

She sprang from her chair with a lightness that came from the inner energy she possessed. Her steps were lively, and she hummed an unfamiliar tune while she gathered her meal from the sideboard in the dining room.

Gaia returned to the table with a plate filled higher than mine had been. Settling down and spreading the napkin on her lap, she looked up at me, then down at my plate, and covered her mouth with her hand and laughed.

"Oops! Didn't know I was eating for two," she laughed.

I smiled but let it pass. I preferred a light breakfast, usually just bread and coffee; she obviously used the early meal to jumpstart herself for the day.

We talked through her chewing and shared laughs about the beach, Americans in Italy, and the differences in the culture between the two countries.

"What part of history are you most interested in?" I asked.

"Europe in the Middle Ages," she said. "I'm focused on historical developments that drove changes in governmental institutions. I care mostly about the evolution of government systems in that period."

I mused about this for a moment, then asked, "Evolution of systems. Tell me more."

"You work for State. I'm sure you know more about it than I do."

Only Americans referred to the U.S. Department of State as 'State;' she was definitely American or had spent time in America, but I set aside my questions on the matter till a later time.

I had not considered her age, or the difference between ours, until that moment. As a student – she hadn't said whether she was undergraduate or in grad school – Gaia was probably in her early 20s; I am thirty years old. Not too much a difference; besides, I didn't intend to make a point of it.

She was right about my work, though. My responsibilities at State required an in-depth familiarity with historical events and my particular field of inquiry – Middle East politics – naturally led to a focus on government systems and social change since World War II, including the forced partition of the region.

"Well, I don't know what you know," I said. "My job does require a lot of time spent on Middle East politics and government systems. And I am the principle translator for the station." I didn't talk about what I was translating or my interrogation responsibilities.

Gaia looked at me without expression, raised a folded bite of prosciutto to her mouth, and chewed on this while staring into my eyes. She didn't say anything at first.

"Middle East," she said without intonation. "Hmm."

A moment passed. She seemed completely disinterested. Or was she actually completed interested. I had to remind myself once again to stop trying to read things into my "subject's" expressions.

"By evolution of government systems," I said to restart the conversation, "do you mean internal changes or external influences?"

"Nation building," she said between bites. She demonstrated quiet confidence in her training and knowledge, so much so that it was easy for her to cut to the chase. "Evolution of government systems" was a convenient byword; but evolution in historical terms was seldom experienced through passive change. More often it was merely a convenient label for nation building.

"Most Westerners think that the colonial period lasted into the 19th century and transitioned to nation building in the 20th century as colonial powers like England, Spain – even America – lost many of their colonies. But nation building was also prominent in medieval times because…"

Here she paused and shook her head a bit. Smiling, she began again.

"I'm rambling, aren't I? Well, it's just that what we're doing in the Middle East – call it nation building if you like – is just a replay of centuries of power shifts throughout the world."

The "we" betrayed her as essentially American, regardless of what other blood she had coursing through her veins.

"But I thought your focus was on Europe during the Middle Ages," I said.

Gaia just smiled through a bite of rustic bread she was chewing, and stared lightly at me.

I let her finish her breakfast while I watched in silent appreciation.

May 17, 2007

I spent a few hours on the beach, just as Umberto had prescribed. The gentle warmth of the sun felt good on my skin, but I imagined it falling instead on the tanned skin of my lover, Gaia. And I imagined her being by my side. I had to rely on my memory and imagination for that, a thought which left me in pain.

In time, bored with the solitude of the beach, I marched up the steps to Casa Albertina and entered my room. The gossamer curtains were drawn apart and a gentle breeze blew past them and lazily wafted into the room.

I sat on the edge of the bed and stared at the floor. After a few moments, I stood and wandered around the bed, making circles circumscribed by the pattern on the carpet. Although this was "my" room, in fact I shared it with others who had resided there in the past, ghosts of other memories, an eerie presence borne out by past guests' journals stacked neatly on the bookshelf by the desk.

I wasn't the only one who captured small moments of his life by scribbling words on a blank page.

Pierre from northern France left his thoughts in the pages of one journal, and Rita from Chicago filled the lined pages of another one.

I had often read through their writings, feeling somewhat like a peeping tom but recognizing that they left their journals in the room so they must have wanted others to read them. I was not so brave. Although I kept the journal my sister had pushed me into, I kept it close, packing it with my things and carrying it back with me when I left Positano.

I also knew that Casa Albertina trafficked in this journal writing game. The owner knew that a guest book unfolded to the present date, filled with cryptic comments tossed off when the guest was hurrying out the door, was only slightly amusing to others. So he encouraged his guests to fill the pages of their own journals – blanks of which he provided to anyone who asked – and leave the books behind for a later visit.

The owner, Piero, was careful to keep a supply of these blank books in a range of colorful covers and sizes. In this way, everyone felt that they were collecting individual thoughts in an individual journal. And the wondrous covers and page designs made the books more interesting to be perused by occasional guests staying in the rooms of Casa Albertina. It was also easy to see how the journals, once left behind, might serve as magnets to draw guests back for future visits, to see Positano again and to add more words to the pages of their own journals.

I walked to the narrow shelf that was perched above the dresser opposite the bed, and picked up a book with a floral theme on the cover. It was made up of about a hundred pages, and as I flipped through them I could see that it was about half full. The writing was consistent, as if only one person rendered the narrative that appeared there.

On the inside the cover, two names were inscribed: Mike and Katherine, and below them in a notation obviously added long after the original entry, there appeared another name: Serena.

I thumbed through the book's pages, noted that the tight, thin strokes of a ball point pen filled the first twenty pages, then yielded to the softer felt-tip ink for the remainder. The first set of pages came from 1988, and the others began with the year 2003. A break in the writing, but from the penmanship I could tell that the author was the same.

Mike's Journal – September 17, 1988

I can't believe the indescribable beauty of this place. Not only Casa Albertina, but Positano itself, and the glory of the sea and sky that stretches out before us. Katherine and I have just been married and we decided to spend our honeymoon in Italy. Exhausted after brief visits to Rome, Florence, and Venice though, we reached Positano and immediately decided to change our plans. We're going to spend the rest of the days we have right here. At Casa Albertina. Sleeping late, eating too much and loving more. I just wish we didn't have to leave – ever.

I read Mike's entry with a slight smile. Forgetting my own situation, my own longing, I took refuge in his joy. So I thumbed through the journal to see how many pages I might be committing to. He had only been to Positano twice and left many pages of memories recorded in the journal.

The first entries followed his wedding to Katherine and captured the pleasant memories of a honeymoon between two people very much in love. Casa Albertina figured prominently in his reminiscences, but his story told the larger tale of their adventures in Positano.

From the first day, we realized that Positano is more vertical than horizontal. It's got a beach, sure, but to get there you have to descend many hundreds of steps or walk a meandering road that switches back and forth down to the sea level below. Going down was full of adventure and laughter, but going back up to the hotel was a real test.

Mike described the gentle heat of the sun on a September morning as he and Katherine lay back on blankets on the beach. Positano's shoreline was composed of black rocks more than sand, so blankets were necessary to shield the body from the absorbed heat of the stones as well as provide a resting place for swimsuit-exposed bodies.

We enjoyed the luxury of sunshine and breeze all morning, returning to the hotel only for a light midday meal. After showering up and changing into clean clothes, we embarked on a walking tour – more like a climbing tour – of the hilly pathways that led up to and down to the Positano beach. The Mediterranean Sea spread out in what seemed like miles below our feet, and the glitter of the sunshine off the water was magical.

I rested the book on my lap for a moment, recalling moments like this with Gaia, including reclining on the beach and hiking up the trails around the town. Mike's recollection was no greater than mine, in fact, he almost repeated things that I had written in my own journal.

This will be our place to remember. Rome was enticing, and Venice and Florence were beautiful, but that so-called Italian triangle sucks up all the tourists who forget, or never knew, of the fragrance of lemon trees, the sparkle of the blue sea, or the twinkle of stars overhead in a place as beautiful as Positano.

My Journal – July 15, 2004

"So," Gaia said. "What's the plan?"

Having finished off the mountain of food on her breakfast plate, she was ready for action. She imbued every word with the vague sensation that the day's activities would amount to a life-defining venture.

"Well, as you said, we should start with the beach. It's early in the day and so it won't be too crowded yet," I said. "Did you bring a bathing suit?"

Gaia cocked her head to the side and a broad smile dawned on her face.

"We're on the Amalfi Coast. In Positano," she said, adding in sing-song, "the most romantic place in Italy!" At that, she winked at me and I could feel the red color rise in my neck and cheeks.

"Why would I not bring a swimsuit?"

Again, the radiant smile.

Standing from her chair but before slipping away, Gaia circled the table and left a kiss on my cheek. She squeezed my hand every so quickly, then dropped it. I rose from my chair and we headed off in the direction of the hallway, tearing apart toward separate rooms as we had done the night before.

Before disappearing around the crook in the corridor, I hazarded a look back. Gaia was walking nonchalantly away, but she turned her chin ever so slightly to her right. She didn't make eye contact, but she anticipated my glance, and was offering a subtle reinforcement.

May 17, 2007

After reading a few pages of Mike's journal, I was be-set with anxiety. It was a hard emotion to place, since nothing had happened in the preceding moments, and nothing appeared in Mike's story to incite that feeling in me. But I had noticed it before, most often when I was alone in Positano. The memories of Gaia flooded back and her absence made my body ache.

I stood from the edge of the bed and shook my head to clear it. Standing still in the middle of the room, I thought back to Mike and Katherine, and how they had shared their love and happiness in the same room where I now shouldered my pain and loss. I gulped with the realization, and nearly wept when I considered the different hands that fate had dealt us. I didn't know Katherine except through Mike's journal entries, but I fantasized about knowing her instead of Gaia. At first the thought was soothing, until I realized that I had never known anyone like Gaia, and I would never want to know anyone other than Gaia again.

I walked out to the lobby of Casa Albertina once more and Piero, the owner, was there chatting with a guest. His lively hand gestures and easy laughter made me smile; I recalled the same impression of him on my first visit to the hotel three years back. He glanced in my direction without interrupting the story he was telling the other couple, nodded to me, then laid his hand on the man's arm, completed his story while wishing him a good day, and turned in my direction.

"Danny," he said, extending his hand. "How are you? I heard you were back."

Piero stared at me for a moment, and I stared back. Wondering what to say to break the silence, I offered, "Always nice to be back at Casa Albertina. Still the most beautiful hotel on the Amalfi Coast."

Piero offered a reluctant smile in reply, shrugged his shoulders, then changed the course of the conversation.

"I have something for you."

Retreating behind the desk, he came back around with a medium-sized box, taped shut and with only my name written on it in the bold strokes of a Sharpie pen. Piero reached out to me with the box, and stood for a moment waiting for me to take it.

I looked at the box, then inquiringly back up at Piero. He shook it gently, once, and extended his arms once more.

"She left it here for you. Gaia. Just about three months ago."

I was filled with a mix of emotions that included confusion and fear, and I felt a wave of terror sweep over me. How could it be that Gaia was here just three months ago and I didn't know it? Was she hiding from me? And why didn't Piero contact me when she was here?

I hesitantly reached for the box and took it from his hands. It was light, but I could tell by the shifting of its contents that there was more than a single thing in the box.

"She said this would explain everything to you," Piero continued, as if anticipating my question about why he hadn't called me. "She didn't want me to call you. She said everything would be alright."

Once more, I stared down at the writing and, without saying anything to Piero, turned and walked back to my room.

I sat on the edge of the bed and gently placed the package on the coverlet beside me. Mike's journal was still splayed open on the pillow by my elbow, but my mind was now on the box that Gaia had left for me. I reached over and flipped shut the cover of Mike's diary, then focused my eyes on the plain brown box.

Knowing that Gaia had been here, at Casa Albertina, stirred the same mix of emotions that I felt in the lobby. My eyes were too dry for tears, but the pace of my heart quickened a bit as I reached over and pulled at the edge of tape that bound the seams of the box together. It was a bridge to the past, I was sure, but I also wondered whether it wasn't a bridge to the present, and to the future, a sudden thought that sent a tingle down my spine and spurred me to action.

From the moment that Piero had proffered the box to me, I had thoughts of doom and loss. But since Gaia had returned to the hotel, to Positano, I began to wonder whether this was a signal that she was looking for me. In spite of the other more conventional ways to find me – and my mind drifted back to the bureaucratic labyrinth of directories in the State

Department – maybe Gaia was sending me a signal in the only way that lovers could communicate.

Nursing both this hope and my multitude of fears, I lifted the flap of the box and opened it slowly. There was a small book inside; the absence of a title on the cover immediately revealed it to be some kind of journal. A bundled stack of letters that had stamps but no postmark, a dried flower from a lemon tree, and a wine-stained glass.

I stared at the contents for a long time, trying to decide which to inspect first and how the knowledge I gained would affect me. The flower and wine glass seemed the most innocent – and likely to cause the least trauma for me – so I withdrew them from the box.

The flower had surely lost its evocative aroma but by putting it close to my nose my imagination allowed me to breath in the scent of a lemon tree. Then I pulled it back and looked it over carefully. I didn't know how old it was. Just because I hadn't seen Gaia in nearly three years, it didn't mean that this flower was that old. Perhaps she had picked it on her more recent visit while collecting artifacts for this time capsule.

I put it down gently on the bedspread, then raised the glass to my eyes. It held a dried out sample of the red wine that had once been in it. There was no scent of wine left, although I twirled it between my fingers as if it still held liquid.

I preferred red wine but I knew that Gaia preferred white. I wondered if this was a clue or a lead to something else. I closely inspected the lip of the glass but failed to detect any evidence of lipstick. Although she was always modest about applying makeup, Gaia liked to add a gloss to brighten her mouth. This would have adhered to the glass, but nothing appeared upon my inspection.

I looked again at the red residue in the bowl and concluded that this glass was one that I had used. Perhaps a last sip of wine shared in her room on our final night in Positano. A glass that I had left behind when I woke to leave the next morning, returning to my own room to shower and dress for the day. But Gaia had kept it, and put it in among her mementos of our time together.

I stopped my survey of the box's contents, struck by the utter mystery of it all. It seemed like the best place to start was in finding out the origin and timing of the package's delivery. So I left the room in search of Piero. Finding him at the front desk, I approached quickly and, without bothering with pleasantries, I asked:

"You said Gaia left this box just three months ago."

"*Sì*, Danny. She handed the box to me personally. When she was here just recently."

"Was it already filled and bound with tape?" I asked.

"*Sì*."

"Was she staying at Casa Albertina that time?"

"No, Danny. Gaia said she was just passing through but wanted to leave this box for you."

"So, she just showed up at your doorstep, Piero, after all this time?" The pitch of my voice rose and I was quite certain that it carried the doubt I felt in my heart.

"No," he replied, then looking down at his hands, continued, "Gaia has been here before, three, maybe four times since 2004 when you met. She…she…" but Piero had nothing more to add.

I became sadder and more confused with this news. Gaia had returned to Casa Albertina a handful of times and, led by Piero's telling of it, I concluded that she was looking for me. Why hadn't she called me, or reached out if she truly wanted to find me?

I had returned myself a handful of times, always in search of her, but until that moment I didn't realize she had done so too. On our last night together, I still thought we had another day before departing. It was then that I was going to get her address and other vital information. I had found the love of my life and while I knew our days in Positano were a precious time together, I had no intention of letting her slip away from me.

Piero paused, swallowed hard, and added, "She was searching for you."

I was confused and hurt. I knew Gaia could find me if she wanted to. Why hadn't she looked me up in the State Department directory? If Gaia wanted to find me there, she could have.

Piero seemed to read my mind, etched no doubt in bold letters across my face.

That was all he said, but I understood; Gaia wasn't looking for me in the State Department registry. She was looking for me in the life that we had shared here.

My Journal - July 15, 2004

I changed more quickly than Gaia and proceeded to the lobby of Casa Albertina to wait for her. My boxer-styled swimsuit – favored by Americans – seemed a bit out of place in a beach culture where men often wore skimpier versions of attire, but it was what I had. Besides, I didn't think I could pull off the speedo look with the confidence that the European men did.

With a light t-shirt sporting a Jimmy Buffett theme and a towel tossed over my shoulder, I was ready for Gaia. I stood for a bit of time, the clock probably moving more quickly than my imagination suggested. After a moment, I realized that my stock-still posture gave away my nervousness. I tried to relax and seem more nonchalant, but the effort only lasted a minute or two.

So, where was she?

A moment later, she entered the lobby and I knew the wait was worth it. Her tanned skin and toned physique would have been enough, but the lacey top she wore could hardly disguise the neon green bikini beneath it. Smiling, as always, she approached and kissed me once more, this time closer to my mouth, and took my hand to begin the trek down to the beach.

"Would it be rude to say you look stunning?" I asked.

Throwing a knowing smile my way, she replied, "It would be rude not to."

Once on the beach we spread our towels beside each other and settled onto the rocky shore. Gaia quickly closed her eyes and struck the pose of someone intent on perfecting her tan. I tried to mimic her composure but frequently stole looks out of the corner of my eye to see her.

Once, when I did this, she smiled, and I knew that she was mindful of my attention. And so the time passed.

* * * *

"Why does democracy get bashed so much?"

I was barely awake but the words brought me to. Gaia was sitting up next to me, leaning back on her hands, her legs lazily stretched out before her. Her question seemed to come out of the blue, but then I wondered whether she had been carrying on a conversation with me that I had only vaguely kept up with while drifting somewhere in the twilight between sleep and wakefulness.

"Well," I began, pushing myself up into the sitting position beside her. I was stalling for time to clear my head of the mist of sleep.

"Democracy is the worst form of government, except for all the others," I offered, relying on a familiar quote to give me time to wake up.

"Winston Churchill," she quickly replied. "But if people have the will and the power to choose their own government, why is that wrong?"

I was careful not to assume that she didn't already have the answer.

"The will and the power is an entitlement that nature granted us," I offered.

"Yes," she picked up the theme, "but we hear arguments around the world, especially in North African nations and the Middle East right now, that democracy is wooden and inflexible. More importantly, we hear not only tyrants but also their people saying that democracy hides corruption, that it is a way of professing equal rights and equal treatment while hoarding the actual power for the privileged few."

So, okay, I realized that Gaia had thought through this very carefully. I didn't have to agree with everything she said – or disagree with it – to know that this woman had deep insights into the geopolitics of the age.

"How about a cool drink?" I offered. Gaia pursed her mouth and looked sternly at me, as if she suspected I was trying to change the subject. I wasn't, and her smile convinced me that she knew this; I was just thirsty and I assumed that she was.

I rose to walk back to the bar at beach level, ordered two glasses of white wine, and returned to our towels. Gaia sipped hers, but then took a deeper draught than I had, managing to finish her glass of wine before I could drain my own.

Standing quickly and looming over me, with the bright sunlight on her shoulders and her face, she said, "Come on. Time for a swim."

Mike's Journal – September 19, 1988

We ate well and drank well last night, and then returned to the room pleasantly exhausted from the day.

We've been sampling our way through the food of Italy, and this proximity to the sea makes it an even more interesting experience. At Ristorante Piscina, we started with *laganelle e ceci*, a chickpea soup with garlic and short pasta noodles, and a drizzle of bright green olive oil on the surface. The loaf of *palata*, a chewy, rustic bread from Campania helped sop up the juices of the soup. When that was done, we moved on to linguine with prawns, swimming in a sauce of butter and white wine and accented with fresh parsley, a pinch of salt, and a sprig of rosemary.

After filling up on all that, we finished off the meal with espresso and limoncello, the succulent lemon-based aperitif that is best when made from the local Sorrento lemons.

After the meal, we returned to the hotel, tired, full, and ready for sleep. As Katherine prepared for bed, I drew the blackout curtains and was asleep before she slipped between the sheets.

When we awoke this morning, it was still very dark in the room. Thinking it was still in the wee hours, I turned toward the clock. Surprised to see that it was 11:30 a.m., I involuntarily leaped from the bed. We had nowhere to go and nothing to do, but I was startled that we had slept so soundly for so many hours.

"Apparently," I said to Katherine as she roused, "Those blackout curtains really work!"

We rose and worked slowly through the morning routine. Me, with a shower and dressing in light summer clothes, Katherine with a shower and longer preparation. I kidded her often that she didn't need to do so much to be beautiful, but she scoffed at me.

"You might not think so," she countered, "if I ever skipped this phase."

I had seen my young wife in many ways, clothed and naked, made up and *au naturel*, and I doubted the need for her preoccupation with hair, make-up, and styling.

May 17, 2007

Piero's explanation left me unsatisfied and distraught. Finding out that Gaia was looking for me, but unwilling to take the usual route to find me, left several layers of doubt in my mind about our time together, the intimacy of our moments, and the future plans that had filled my mind in those days back in July 2004.

I sat on the edge of the bed and returned to my thoughts. Yes, I had already entertained many ideas of a future with Gaia. She was a student in the States and I worked for the State Department. Why couldn't it work out?

But did she have the same thoughts?

I was sure that Gaia felt the same toward me. All of which made her sudden disappearance three years ago all the more confusing.

I looked down at the box again and withdrew the bundled stack of letters. I couldn't remember all the intricacies of what her handwriting looked like, except for one thing. Back when we were together, Gaia had scrawled a little note on the bedside pad of paper, a note to tell me when I woke that she would be back in a moment. I recall the flourish of the "y" she added at the end of my name, and saw this same flourish on the envelopes stacked in the box.

I lifted the packet and, thumbing through the pile, I could see that they were neatly arranged in chronological order. I took the first one, the oldest one dated June 14, 2005, and turned it over to open the flap. Sealed, but not stamped, and clearly not planned for mailing.

Scrawled neatly across the envelope's flip side was this:

"To Danny, the only true love of my life"

A violent shudder went down my spine. I now knew that she felt as strongly as I did. I stared dumbly at the paper in my hands, anxious to read it but nervous about what I would find out. What secret was buried in these letters; in fact, what secret had she kept from me while we were together?

I gently pulled on the flap and lifted the letter out.

Gaia's Letter – June 14, 2005

Danny, I love you.

Her handwriting was elegant, a small script that had easy rolls and languorous tails. The tall letters were graceful, the loops of each letter perfectly rounded. The appearance added luxury to the words as I read them.

I have been looking for you, as I know you have been looking for me. I just want you to know that I will never lose you. This time apart is necessary, and although I know you'll understand when you hear my story, I can't tell it to you at this time.

But I wanted you to know how precious those days were with you in Positano. It's a magnificent place, to be sure, but you made it even more perfect. I never thought that I would find someone who fit me so well, with whom I could relax so easily, and whom I was certain would accept every decision that I made.

I'll tell you my whole story, in time, and I hope that you will not blame me for my silence. And I hope you will understand why I had to leave you one day early during our time together. It broke my heart, not just to depart without explaining, but to leave and be without your embrace, your love, and your gentle laughter.

It comes from my training. What I am doing is very important, and I hope to be able to use my knowledge and my experience to make a difference in this world.

But you should know from this moment on, if you didn't already figure it out when we were together, that I love you. Now, and forever.

Gaia.

Gaia's Journal – July 15, 2004

I'd like to spend some time with you, my little book, but I'm in a hurry.

Last night I met a man who seems so nice, so interesting, such perfect company. We decided that we would spend some time together today. I've just finished breakfast and we're going out to the beach, and I don't want to keep him waiting, so I'll just jot down a few thoughts.

His name is Danny; he's an American. Well, that's okay (ha ha). We were both sitting on the terrazza here at the hotel and he started talking to me. I really wasn't interested at first; I wanted to focus on my responsibilities. Yeah, sure, I was going to have some fun before returning, but "fun" was going to be more like walking on the beach, drinking too much wine (well, we did that too!). I didn't think fun was going to include meeting some guy.

It's too early to tell, but I think I like him. We're going to spend some time together (he's here for five days just like me) and I'll just have to see what develops.

Oh, yeah, and he works for the State Department. Hmm. Well, that's okay too, I guess.

Mike's Journal – September 19, 1988

We spent some time touring Italy before landing in Positano but BOY am I glad we did. This cliffside oasis has to be one of Mother Earth's greatest creations. The town is perched on the side of a tremendous hill, or mountain, you might say, hanging onto a ribbon of highway taped to a sheer cliff of mountain. The stone buildings, homes, and hotels seem to be glued to the slope of the cliff, and bound together like some great tapestry hanging from the blue sky above.

Positano faces south, or a bit southwest, so we can watch the sun glide overhead until it dips into the Mediterranean at sunset. The azure sky with silky white clouds stretch out into infinity on the west, meeting the sea at a horizon too far away to imagine.

There are some smells that remind me of a typical Italian village, but the aroma of Sorrento lemons ripening on the trees and the fragrance of basil and rosemary that grows in bushes outside of every restaurant makes the fragrant air almost possible to eat. Even the pungent aroma of fish around the cluster of fishing boats at the shore adds to the pleasure of Positano.

I called the rest of the hotels on our honeymoon itinerary because Katherine and I have extended our stay here. We will just lay by the water, eat when we're hungry, go to bed when we're tired, and wake when we're rested. I do believe that the people of the Amalfi Coast live in God's own Eden. And we'd like to stay here as long as we're welcome.

My Journal – July 15, 2004

As the sun rose higher and the air warmed up, we decided to go inside to let our skin rest and our eyes adjust to softer light. Leaving our blankets on the stony beach, Gaia and I stood and turned toward the café that was shaded by the green and white striped awning that loomed above it.

Gaia stumbled a bit on the rocks and reached out for my hand. I held it gently and smiled. It elicited a short giggle from her as she steadied her feet. We reached the café and immediately felt the cooler air on our sun-warmed skin. Settling into welcoming chairs by the perimeter, we enjoyed the shade and cool air of the fan above our heads while still keeping an eye on the sea and the beachgoers crowding the shoreline.

For a few moments we were silent, and the silence comforted me a great deal. If this was what I was meant to find here, on R&R in Positano, then this holiday was bound to be life-changing. Just sitting beside Gaia, our arms dangling over the arms of the chairs with our fingers entwined, I felt that we had already passed through to some other plane in our relationship. Barely twelve hours before we were still strangers, but there was a stillness and a comfort in our closeness. I let my thumb lightly stroke the back of her hand and got a similar gesture in response. Gaia turned her smile toward me and squeezed my hand.

When the waiter approached, she ordered a limoncello and I ordered a Campari and soda. When the man retreated from our table, Gaia and I returned our gaze to the beach but our hands remained connected.

"Have you ever had this?" she asked, holding out the glass of bright yellow liquid. With my eyes still on the beach and blue sea, I at first thought she meant us. Have I ever had such a wonderful closeness and a natural connection to someone? No, I hadn't. But when I looked over at her, I realized that Gaia was holding up the glass of limoncello and was much more in the moment than I.

"No, not yet," I laughed, and took the drink from her to sample it.

It was a luscious elixir, full bodied but sporting a bright, syrupy lemon flavor. The iconic aroma of the local Sorrento lemons filled my nostrils even before I lifted the glass to my lips. Taking a sip, I let it linger a moment on my tongue, then I swallowed it. It was a wonderful taste, something so fitting for this beach-side resort, a velvety smooth tonic that was perfect under the Mediterranean sun.

"Have you ever had this?" I asked Gaia, offering my Campari and soda to her. It was every bit the opposite of her limoncello, a reddish liquid with a pleasantly bitter effect on the mouth.

"Eww," she said after sipping at the glass. "That's awful!"

"No, it's not," I protested, although I was slightly certain that this would be her first impression. I recalled my first introduction to the liquor, when I was similarly put off by it, but soon grew to like it.

"Campari is naturally bitter, but it comes in a class of bitters that are best served as a hot weather drink to cool you off."

Lifting her limoncello, Gaia countered, "Yeah, well I like my hot weather drink just fine!" And she sipped at the glass while a smile played across her lips.

It was fun relaxing here this afternoon. We had already had a few hours of sun, so sitting in the cool of the shade felt invigorating. Gaia suggested staying there a bit longer, "having another drink" she added, but we asked for the menu first.

A short wait was rewarded when the waiter returned with two platters, one topped with grilled vegetables and the other a sampling of cheese, olives, and deep fried calamari. We dove into the grilled eggplant, zucchini, asparagus, and peppers, then added broad slices of asiago cheese and crumbled Parmigiano, green and shriveled black olives, and calamari to our already heaping plates.

I had learned on previous trips to Italy that they take their meals seriously. The platter that we were working our way through would be considered just an appetizer here, so I reserved some appetite for what would inevitably follow.

After a few more moments, Gaia relented. Full of the delicious morsels already, she leaned back in the chair as if to say *basta*, "enough!" in Italian

"There's more," I said.

She gave me a quizzical look, not sure what I meant, whether it involved food or something else. So I had to laugh. Her look nearly invited me to change the "menu" for the afternoon, but I resisted - - for the moment.

"I think the *cameriere* is waiting for the rest of our order."

Gaia's eyes grew at the thought of the waiter returning with more food, so I tried to explain.

"Italians are serious about their food, which is why it all tastes so good. But they're serious about their meals, too. They don't like to walk and eat, for example, so you'll seldom see an Italian walking around munching on a sandwich or an American 'wrap,' and they won't tolerate fast food.

"So a proper meal has several dishes. Just watch," I added, then turned and nodded to the waiter.

He came to the table and stood silently waiting for the next course to be ordered.

"Another thing: Italians don't like to be hurried. So when we placed our order for the antipasto platter, he wasn't expecting that to be the last thing in the meal, and he was okay letting us relax with the tender bites and let us wait till we were ready to order more."

Almost on a dare, I summoned some mental notes I had made of the local cuisine and turned toward the waiter.

"*Vogliamo baccalà alla napoletana.*" This is a local favorite, salt cod that is floured then fried, then served with tomatoes, garlic, capers and olives, sometimes with raisins and toasted pine nuts.

"*Sì, signore. E un po di 'fusilli alla vesuviana?' Sul lato?*" offered the waiter. I remembered the recipe for the fusilli, a twisted pasta cooked in a sauce reminiscent of a beef stew, but held up my hand to suggest that, maybe, that was too much.

Gaia watched with a blend of curiosity and sort of wondrous horror at the amount of food.

"*Un po,*" I replied, "just a bit," tamping my right hand down softly as if to indicate only a small portion.

The waiter repeated, "*Sì, sul lato,*" and then I realized that the phrase *sul lato* meant on the side.

"*D'accordo,*" I said, agreeing with the suggestion.

Gaia continued her look of awe.

"You speak Italian, too?"

"Only a bit, *un po,* I said with a laugh. But I was pleased that I had impressed her.

Her raised eyebrows were enough reward for me.

"*Ana muejb,*" she responded. Now it was time for my eyes to widen. That sounded like a variant of Pashto, and because I recognized it as the translation for "I'm impressed," I knew that it must be. It was time for my eyebrows to raise, as I pondered the breadth of this young woman's knowledge.

Leaning back after the brief conversation, Gaia's eyes twinkled, green flecks sparkling, and her mouth moved into a satisfied smile. Her attempt to demur failed, and she flashed a contented look back at me.

Another round of drinks was inevitable, then another, as we sat back in our chairs and relaxed in the breeze that wound about the tables there.

For a moment that seemed longer than it probably was, we stared into each other's eyes. Hers seemed to glow; mine nearly teared up.

Relaxing after the meal was finished, I stared out at the crystal waters beyond the pebble beach, for a moment taken in by the beauty of it all. I couldn't believe how happy I was just then, and realized that Gaia was the central source of the blissful feeling that I was enjoying.

A blaze of sunlight reflected off the water and momentarily caught my eye, inducing me to look away slightly, and when I did I saw that Gaia was watching me. For how long, I didn't know. But when she caught my eye, she smiled – a warm, satisfied smile

– and I realized that we were both drawing on each
other's energy.

Gaia's Letter – July 16, 2005

Dearest Danny,

Last year at this time we were together in Positano. Now, as I look out on the waters of the Mediterranean Sea, it seems so strange. You're not here, and that makes all the difference to me.

I stopped reading for a moment and looked again at the envelope. Just like Gaia's letter from June 14, this one had my name scrawled on the front but there was no postmark or stamp, or other evidence of its origin.

I laugh whenever I think of the stories you told, and the happy times we spent sipping limoncello - - oh, that's right, you like that red stuff! - - but I also cry alone at night from missing you. The strength of your embrace, the warmth of your skin next to mine, even the sound of your breathing next to my ear as we lay in the bed. I remember it all with sweet clarity.

Right now, I'm sitting in a café sipping strong coffee and watching happier people go by the window. Well, let me restate that.

Meeting you made me happier than I've ever been, so it's not true that all these people are happier than I am. Sure, the ones who are holding their lovers' hands may be, but not all.

Life is hard in this world, and many people live lives of desperation and want. The love they have in their hearts may be the only strength they can call on. Just like me.

I just wish I could put my arms around your neck and look into your eyes. That would be enough for now.

More later,

Love, Gaia

I wiped tears from my eyes as I reread the words "I'm sitting in a café." Why couldn't she tell me where? Was she hiding her location, or did that just not seem worth the mention? Gaia's out there somewhere, wishing she were with me, and I am here in Positano where this all started – wishing I was with her.

I truly don't understand.

May 17, 2007

I read the letter again, searching for more than was written on the page. My hands dropped to my lap, still clutching the paper between my fingers as I stared off to the far horizon, the watery distance of the Mediterranean, the same backdrop whose blue waves and brilliant sunshine helped me fall in love with Gaia.

Her letter filled in few details that I didn't know, hadn't known, since that day in 2014 when I returned to her room to find her gone.

I remember stepping through the doorway, expecting to see her done with her shower, dressed, and ready to go. By then the sun shone brightly through the open shutters while a wisp of cool morning air slipped between the barely open French doors leading out to her balcony.

But she wasn't in bed, so I went to find her in the shower. With no sound of water running, I thought she might be tending to more private business, so instead of pushing the door open and embarrassing her, I listened carefully for any sounds. Hearing none,

I knocked. Getting no response, I turned the door-knob and let myself in.

The bathroom was a bit rumpled as always – Gaia's surroundings always seemed to reflect to the casual relationship she had with life – but there was no sign of her. A towel was on the floor and a spent makeup bottle on the sink, which was when I noticed it.

The door to the cabinet next to the sink was ajar. Pulling it open with my fingers, I saw that it was empty except for the various toiletries that were put in the room by the maid. There was nothing that I would identify with Gaia. I hadn't checked her inventory of personal effects, so I didn't know what I should find, but there were clearly no items that belonged to her alone.

I spun on my heels and went through the door into the bedroom area. A sudden breeze blew the door open and whipped around my head, then died down. I pulled the door to the armoire open and saw nothing. No clothes, no suitcase; only empty hangers scattered carelessly across the hanging bar and the floor.

My first reaction was that I was in some sort of time warp. I even wondered momentarily if I had imagined it all, but that wasn't possible. Gaia's body, the scent of her hair, her smile, her eyes…everything, were too real to me. I could even still call up the feeling of her lips against mine just one hour before.

With the recollection fresh in my mind, I returned to the present, shook my head lightly and returned to the letter on my lap. The memories of that morning were held captive in my mind as if I had lived them just yesterday. They were the only firm memories I had of Gaia, painful and hopeful at the same time, although admittedly too few. Memories that had sustained me for the last three years, until I was handed that box by Piero.

My mouth twisted into one of pain and sadness as I thought back. Reaching into the front pocket of my pants, I withdrew a crumpled envelope that I had carried with me every day since July 2004. It bore my name in the neat scrawl that was Gaia's, and I carefully lifted out the one page note inside. She had left it for me that morning, a memento that I didn't discover until I had scoured the room for clues. Gaia had leaned it against the table lamp next to the bed.

The brief note said only:

"Danny, I love you but I must leave for now. I hope you understand.

"We will be together again, if you will still have me.

"Love, Gaia"

My Journal - July 15, 2004

I'm writing this during an unwanted break from Gaia in the afternoon. I hope to have time to add more later.

After a larger meal than I had planned for, and a few rounds of drinks, Gaia and I returned to the beach and the towels that we had left there. By then, the sun was high in the sky and the heat of the day had risen also. We both donned sunglasses to ward off the searing light, and assumed our positions of sun worshippers. But this time we intertwined our hands and rested in the comfort of the shared embrace.

The day became hotter and hotter. We were expecting a more bearable temperature, and maybe a small storm, but rain showers are infrequent here. About an hour after returning to our place on the beach, Gaia and I gave up and decided – probably under the influence of food and drink – that we should retire to the hotel.

She was up and on her feet first, always more spry and energized than me, and we gathered up our few belongings and trekked back up the beach and took the long climb to Casa Albertina.

Tossing her towel over her shoulder to free her hand, Gaia reached out for mine.

"Well, the sun feels great, but that was quite enough heat for one day," she said.

I smiled back but had little to say. I was enjoying the easy way that we were together and held back on words so as not to spoil it.

Our entwined hands swung lazily between us as we mounted the steps back up to the hotel. Once inside the lobby and safe in shade for once, my eyes slowly adapted from the brilliant glare of the sun to the dimmer light of the lobby. Gaia pulled at my hand and swung me around to face her. Leaving a warm kiss on my lips she smiled not so demurely, and said she needed to shower.

"And there's only room for one in there," she added playfully. I had a room much like hers and knew there was room in the shower for two people, if they wanted to share intimate space, but I knew her comment was meant to protect her for now, so I let it drop. I definitely didn't want to overplay my hand.

Stepping lightly away toward the corridor, Gaia turned back, waved a little girl wave, and said, "I'll see you around six, on the terrace."

Six? That was three hours away! Okay, so maybe she needed a shower and perhaps a little nap. But I knew I couldn't fill up three hours without her. It would feel like ten!

* * * *

Later this evening:

Well, I was right, in a way, and wrong. The three hours did seem like an eternity, but I survived it. I too headed off to the shower to wash the sun and sand from my body, then spent some time adding notes to this journal. I can't help smiling through the writing, and at one point I even thought of my sister. She convinced me to keep this journal, saying that I could reread the entries when I returned to Afghanistan and the memories would soften me.

Boy, if she had only known!

Gaia appeared promptly on the terrazza at six o'clock. Of course, I was already waiting there...I couldn't hide my eagerness and didn't want to miss a moment with her.

She cleaned up well, as the saying goes. Her hair was pulled back in a long ponytail and glistened in the evening light. With the sun on her face as she exited the lobby, I could see the bronze skin tone, her sparkling eyes, and the light gloss of pink lipstick on my mouth. She wore a light lavender-colored patterned dress with square-cut scooping neckline, and a white beaded bracelet dangling from her left wrist.

Little makeup other than the ever-present lipstick, and no other jewelry, but Gaia looked like a million bucks. She stepped toward me quickly, but my mind and imagination slowed time down to a trickle. I watched as she reached up with both hands, putting one on each side of my face, and drew my mouth to hers. It was a soft, earnest kiss, showing a bit of passion, but reserved enough not to embarrass me here in a public spot.

I couldn't suppress the welling of blood and emotion that swept over me. I smiled broadly, put my arms around her slender waist and leaned back in for another kiss. Gaia obliged, but then pulled back, smiled, and put her index finger up to my lips instead.

"We have time," was all she said.

Gaia's Journal – July 15, 2004

Oh, Danny, Danny, Danny. This is too much fun. The afternoon in the sun was hot, but this evening
already seems like it's going to be hotter.

You've returned to your room so I just have a moment to enter some thoughts. I told you that we'd meet at six. Please don't be late!!

Thanks for making my blood run hot and making this one of the most wonderful days of my life. And, no, I'm not influenced by the drinks at lunch. Well, maybe, but it's like my soul feels a rush of emotion whenever I see you. The waves from the sea outside make that feeling all the more real, like the Mediterranean is pouring over me and filling me with a warm tingly feeling.

How could you do that? I've known men before – I'm not a child. But the suddenness of this feeling has taken me over. Do you feel that way? Or am I just a vacation girlfriend?

I've also learned from my father how good a good man can be. Even while you heat my blood up, you seem to fit that noble role. Oh, God, I hope I'm not just a vacation girlfriend!

My Journal – July 15, 2004

We decided to have dinner here tonight, at Casa Albertina. The food from the region focuses on seafood, a natural for this coastal area, and we already knew that the hotel had much to offer.

I'm going to sneak in a few thoughts while you're back in your room. You said you had to get something, leaving me here on the terrazza. Hurry back!

Piero must have seen romance in the works, because he set aside the perfect table on the terrace. Set just for two, with the chairs snuggled together and both facing the sea.

Gotta quit. Why did you have to go back to your room?

Mike's Journal – September 19, 1988

We've been sleeping late, lying in the sun most of the day, and taking hiking trips through the hills that surround Positano. It's magical. I think it would even be magical without Katherine by my side, but this is the absolute best.

Since the Amalfi Coast is known for its seafood, we decided to sample as much as possible. Last night we shared a platter of *frutta di mare*. Kat smiled a worrisome grin and asked if this wasn't too much of a gamble.

"What's in it?" she asked me.

I just shrugged my shoulders. I have no idea what they think belongs in this dish. So I asked the waiter. He too shrugged his shoulders, although I had to laugh because it seemed like his gesture was so much more conversational than mine. He went on to say that *frutta di mare* means fruit of the sea. Clams, mussels, tiny sardines and other fish, less identifiable forms of sea life... So, not really sure what we were in for, I decided to shrug my shoulders back, and this time I think I got it just right because the waiter laughed with me.

But before the fish arrived, we were served bowls of *soffritto*, a Neapolitan soup that featured various bits of meat, flavored with herbs and tomato sauce, and spiced up with red pepper flakes. A basket of thick crusty bread still hot from the oven was delivered alongside the *soffritto*, to dip and sop up the juices.

Next came *insalata Caprese*, a leaf salad spruced up with tomatoes, mozzarella, and fresh leaves of basil, and dressed with a deep green extra virgin olive oil.

Finally, a steaming platter arrived, piled high with shellfish, shimmering little sardines, mollusks of various shapes and sizes, and even pinkish red baby shrimp. It was clearly too much food for two people, especially after we had just consumed two other courses, but another bottle of Fiano wine was brought to the table and waiter said, "*Mangia!*"

So we did. It was all amazing. The flavors were so fresh and real it was easy to understand why it was called the fruit of the sea. Although Kat (and even

I) occasionally inspected the next forkful with skepticism.

A fine meal and two bottles of wine later – yeah, we drank that much – and we had to take a walk. It didn't last that long (neither could we) but we stood out on the railing that separated the restaurant from the steep slope down to the sea and took in the twinkling lights of the fishing boats, the glimmer of the moon on the water, and the tinkling sound of soft bells in the distance.

After a moment of silence, Kat – still looking away at the sea – said, "We should bring our children here someday."

It was a throwaway line and shouldn't have startled me, but my eyes popped open at the thought. We're here on our honeymoon and while we were practicing "baby making," staring off into a family in the future was still daunting.

Hmmm, could that be why she was so hungry tonight. At dinner, I mean?

Gaia's Letter – May 9, 2006

Dear Danny,

I'm back and I'm looking for you, but of course you're not here. Why would you be on my own schedule?

I need to find you, but I won't – can't – look for you at the State Department. I need to find you here, in Positano.

It seems so long, now, since we were together. I haven't known any man since you. What about you?

I had to stop reading for a moment. Working my way through Gaia's letters was both encouraging and deflating, and I wanted to answer the questions that she posed in her letters. Why didn't she call me, and ask me these things on the phone? Of course I would have told her that there had been no other woman. But if she has no other man, why won't she come back to me.

I glanced at the top of the letter again. It was written a little over a year ago. And, yes, I knew that this was two years since we had met.

She has some deep secret that she won't share. She's not married (or is she?) and has no boyfriend. She can't be running from the author-ities, can she? It must be more than the schooling she talked about.

My head shakes and my eyes water thinking about it.

When we're together again, I will be done and I will explain everything. You must trust me, though, my love.

Forever, Gaia

May 17, 2007

Reading. Wondering. Tortured by what is written and what doesn't appear on the pages of these letters and in Gaia's journal.

I clutched Gaia's last letter to my chest but I was tiring from the effort. I knew that this collection would bring me closer to her, but when would it bring her to me?

I rose from the bed and stepped toward the balcony of my room. The sea seemed infinite and eternal, in a way that my love for Gaia did. It was the same scene that I had shared with Gaia, the same glittering waves, the same bright sun, the same white noise of beachgoers romping by water's edge.

Even the aromas were the same. The narcotic fragrance of tarragon, basil, and rosemary, flowers and fresh lemons all blended into a symphony of edible senses. The smell of grilled meat and steamed seafood wafted up from the restaurants that hung onto the cliffside below Casa Albertina, and brought back memories of our dinners together.

"Oh, my God," Gaia exclaimed that night at Da Marco's! This is fantastic!" Gaia attacked her meals with a gusto that matched her bubbly nature. All food was fantastic, all wine was wonderful... I wondered if she would attack me with the same gusto.

Just then I realized that she had read my mind because she looked across her pasta-laden fork and smiled mischievously at me.

I turned back to the bed and laid the letter down softly on the pillow. I knew Gaia was not actually in that box and no matter how much pain or solace her writing gave me, I needed a break.

Passing through the door into the quiet hallway, I found Piero just turning the corner.

"Why can't you help me find her?" I asked abruptly.

Piero looked at me with pain etched across his face.

"She doesn't leave an address," he said at first, "at least not a true one."

My brow scrunched up at this last comment and he knew he'd have to share more.

"I know you're looking for her, Danny, and I know that this is the most important thing in your life. So, the second time that she came back to Casa Albertina, I asked her if I could help. She said no, and just looked away at the sea. She seemed so sad, so distant.

"I told her that I liked to keep home addresses for our guests, making up the point that we like to send out invitations and brochures. Gaia knew better and saw right through my ploy, but she smiled back and agreed."

"So, you have an address?"

Piero looked earnestly into my eyes.

"Yes, but no.

"Gaia did give me an address and I was going to send it to you. But first, Umberto found something that she had left behind and mailed it to her. It came back."

Piero was silent for a moment.

"It came back, Danny. She didn't give me a true address."

"How can I reach her, Piero?"

He shrugged and held his hands, palms up, out in front of him.

"I don't know, Danny. I can tell from her visits that she wants you too. Why would she not contact you?"

His question seemed unfair to me, but mostly because I didn't have an answer to a very reasonable query.

Did I say something that went wrong? Did I miss something that I should have caught? In her voice, her eyes? Her embrace?

A long sigh slipped from my lips and I averted my gaze from Piero. He laid his hand on my shoulder in consolation, but that didn't help.

My Journal – July 15, 2004

Alright, I'm writing these notes as we sit here in the restaurant. I know that I can't capture the myriad dishes if I wait too long to write them down, so I want to get it right.

We're splurging and having dinner at Da Vincenzo, a favorite of the locals but less well known among the tourists. Piero told us that this place has the best and truest Neapolitan food, but also features the wines and dishes from the larger region of Campania. So…what the heck!

Gaia is having a glass of Greco di Tufo, a local white wine that is zesty and smooth. I've long heard about Taurasi, a red wine made from the Aglianico grape, and I couldn't resist sampling here while in Campania.

Marco, the talkative and bombastic owner of the restaurant, hovered over us and all his guests. His cheerful smile and gentle coaching as to the best food in the establishment – "It's all good!" he would say – added to the festive atmosphere.

Without even waiting for our order, Marco brought a plate of *crostini alla napolitana*. The bread slices are oiled just as with more common versions, but here the chopped tomato, basil, garlic, and anchovies are mounded on the bread before it goes in the oven. A quick warming under the broiler and the *crostini* is served right to the table before the oil even cools.

Marco insisted on serving *sartù di riso*, a rice timbale stuffed with meat, chicken, peas, onions…so many things that I can't even remember. But it was the most beautiful dish I had ever experienced.

"Don't you want to talk to me?" Gaia interrupted, but with a smile.

"Oh, sorry," I said, and closed the journal.

* * * *

Later tonight:

While Gaia was getting ready for bed, I was able to return to writing. But I'll have to make it quick; I'm in her room and "getting ready" includes getting ready for me.

Gaia's Journal – July 15, 2004, late night

Oh, Danny, too much food, too much wine, too much loving…well, maybe not too much of that.

You're worn out (ha ha! I hope I helped with that) and after all that pleasure you fell asleep. You're on your side facing me in bed, with your head deep into the feather pillow, but your eyes are firmly closed and your soft breathing makes me quite sure you're asleep.

I'm worn out too (thank you!) but I can't sleep. This is the most alive – the most awake – I've been my entire life.

Okay…don't wake! You just stirred and reached your hand across my waist. I brushed the back of it with my fingers and your eyes fluttered. Don't wake! I want to just watch you there.

You make it so easy to love you, Danny. From last night and your awkward approach (yeah, sorry buddy, it wasn't that smooth!) to tonight as you wrapped me in your arms, I was on a journey that I knew would not end. It won't, will it?

Your laughter at the amount of food at Da Vincenzo's and your slurping of the wine – was that Taurasi good? – I recorded them all in my memory bank to call up when I'm away from you. But, no, that's not something we're going to talk about right now.

You just stirred again and this time opened your eyes. I had to slip the journal away quickly, but when you shut your eyes again and fell back asleep I pulled it out.

Your hair is curly black but there are signs of gray at the temples. I just realized that I haven't asked you how old you are. Well, that's fair. I haven't told you my age either. Just for the record, I'm twenty-two, but you'll know everything about me soon enough.

I think you already know the most important parts of me.

Mike's Journal – September 19, 1988

It's our last night in Positano. I can't believe we have to go. Being with Katherine is always enough for me, but being with her in Positano is positively other worldly.

We went for a walk on the beach since this is our final evening. It's like the moon scattered sparkles on the water, and the gods lit up the red, blue, and yellow lights on the houses in the slope behind us, like visible music. Turning left, the Mediterranean spreads out before us like a glittering carpet that is constantly fluttering in the waves.

Turning right, my eyes are drawn upward to the sloping hillside, the curving perimeter roadway, and the stone houses, restaurants, and shops that cling to this incredible slice of earth like the treasure in a science fiction story.

It truly must be a fiction. Katherine and I have fallen even deeper in love in this place, deeper than I could have imagined. And I have Positano to thank for that. The food, the wine, the scenes that lay before us. Even Casa Albertina played a part in making this the perfect honeymoon.

Piero gave me this blank book when we checked in and I wasn't quite sure what to do with it. But he must know that the magic of this place inspires even average people like me to wax poetic. And as he requested, I'll leave this book with him. He promises that it will be waiting for me and Kat when we return to his hotel.

What a great lure to come back!

My Journal – July 16, 2004, morning

I've returned to my own room while you shower and get ready for the day. So I get to take a few minutes and inscribe some thoughts and memories of you while you're busy.

Although writing about our time together won't really be necessary. Everything about you is seared into my memory. But since I started this journal I can't seem to leave it incomplete.

Gaia, who are you?! You're amazing, wonderful, beautiful, and so passionate. I don't think this is just Positano talking, although I have to admit that the wonder of this place has ramped up my perceptions of pleasure. But, no, it's you.

Today, I want to find out more about you. I know your voice, your eyes, your smile, even the funny crease that deepens in your cheeks when you laugh out loud. And I've discovered things about your body that are also seared into my memory.

But I want to know who you are, where you come from and where you're going. Of course we're going to figure out how far away we live from each other – and find a way to shorten the distance.

Wait, I'm moving too fast. If I interrogate you about your life (and loves?) I'll probably scare you off. I've survived the clumsy meeting and you still let me into your life; now I have to be careful not to screw up the next few days we have together.

Oh, one more thing: Marco was right. That *sartù di riso* was to die for. It was far too much for us to finish, still he brought us *anginetti* (little sugar cookies) and coffee afterward – he said "You have to stay awake!" as if he knew something about us.

We walked slowly back to Casa Albertina, holding hands and occasionally stopping to take in the view and share kisses that grew ever more intimate. Umberto was at the desk when we came through the entrance. He smiled lightly and nodded to us as we passed. His head also tracked our path as, this time, we didn't split up to walk down different corridors.

You gripped my hand just a little bit more firmly as we reached the break in the path, and guided me in the direction of your room. There we spent a night of, well, you know the rest.

This morning, you told me to give you an hour. I don't know why that's necessary. I'm done in ten minutes and I'm anxious to see you. I suggested just returning to your room while you prepped for the day, but you demurred.

"A girl's gotta have some time to get ready," you said. I offered to just sit quietly on the bed and read, but you wagged your finger at me, shaking your head left and right.

So, here I am. Alone for now.

May 17, 2007

I returned to my room and picked up another one of Gaia's letters. This one was dated September 4, 2006. Not very long ago.

My journey into the past – was it still "our" past – had become more difficult and scary for me. I knew too little about her; I thought back to that day in July 2004 when I resolved to ask Gaia about her life. Worried that I would ask too much, I deferred some of the questions. I wanted to keep our time together one of intimacy and fun, not a search for real-life experiences or the unburdening of secrets or family stories.

But now I wondered if I had asked too little. I even wondered whether my failure to be inquisitive had convinced her that I wasn't really interested in a long-term relationship.

That thought made me shiver. Had my careful act of keeping things simple, and not complicating our vacation romance, driven her away, fearing that to me she was only a brief tryst? Nothing could be farther from the truth, but if this is what she thought – and this is what made her leave and be reluctant to contact me – had I totally screwed up my life already?

Gaia, how do I tell you that I wanted you then and I want you now? How do I get that message to you?

"Piero," I shouted when I raced to the lobby. I had hastily written everything about me, phone number, address, email accounts for both home and work, cell number. As I inspected the meager account of my life scribbled on this slip of paper, I wondered why there wasn't more I could write down.

I couldn't say "Gaia, I love you. Please call me." Those words were too personal and, anyway, might not be necessary if this note ever got to Gaia.

I handed it to Piero. He took the paper without expressing any emotion.

"She knows you're looking for her," he said of Gaia.

"But I want her to look for me."

"She is," he replied, and I was reminded of Piero's earlier explanation that Gaia had to find me in Positano, not in life. My face burned red with frustration. That didn't make any sense. If she wanted to find me, and I her, why would she not just call my cell phone or my office at the State Department?

"Please keep this," I told Piero. "And give it to Gaia when she comes here next. And please tell her to contact me."

Piero just nodded.

At that moment, I thought about asking him how much it would cost to stay full time at Casa Albertina, waiting for Gaia to return. But not only could I not afford the money, I couldn't afford to leave my post in Afghanistan.

I went back to my room, hoping to be strengthened enough to read through more of Gaia's letters. Still worried about the contents but becoming more anxious to find out what she had to say – that she wrote down but couldn't send to me – I tore the envelope open.

My Journal – July 16, 2004, evening

Gaia's in the shower and I'm propped up on her bed writing to you, my journal. Yes, she let me stay in the room while she got ready. Maybe that's progress!

We had another great day. We started on the beach, splitting our time equally between sunning and walking. A long splash in the sea cooled us off and rinsed the sweat and beach sand from our skin, and revived us for another hour of tanning.

The midday meal was simple. We returned to the same beachside café we had used yesterday. Wine, of course, came first followed by a salad of tomato wedges, mozzarella, and red onions sliced into slivers. A tangy balsamic vinegar and succulent extra virgin olive oil were all that was needed for dressing, and we ate greedily and cleaned our plates.

Deep-fried calamari followed. In the States, this dish is usually accompanied by a bowl of marinara sauce to dip the squid into, but here the food is so good that sauces are often omitted from the table.

That led to another glass of wine, a double espresso for each of us, and *tiramisu*, to finish off the meal. That should have put us both into a deep slumber, so instead of returning to the beach, we decided to retreat to the breezy comfort our Gaia's room.

We tossed our swimsuits onto the floor and verified that – in fact – the shower was large enough for two.

A light sheet was the only thing needed to cover us for a nap this afternoon, filled with food and flush with excitement. We slept soundly until just now, about six o'clock. You've gone off to the shower again, this time warding me off with that wagging finger, and I'm sitting up in bed to scribble some thoughts.

"Why don't you go shower?" you called out from behind the slightly open door.

As I made my way in your direction, you poked your head around the door and said:

"Don't you think you'd find clean clothes and shaving things back in your own room?"

"I could bring them here," I suggested with a sly smile.

That wagging finger again.

Mike's Journal – September 19, 1988

Okay, rest easy now, Mikey. Kat just told me that she's not pregnant. Not that I don't want kids but, boy, not quite yet! Whew!

It took me a while to find the journal because I had already moved it from the nightstand to the book shelf. But I didn't want to leave the entry without an explanation.

But, with Katherine, I certainly hope to have children!

Gaia's Letter – September 4, 2006

My dear Danny,

I'm writing to you from Kabul right now. I supposed that comes as a shock, but I'll try to explain. It has nothing to do with my studies in Medieval government systems.

Do you remember the discussion we had about nation building and evolution of government systems?

Well, I'm not here because I'm a student, because I'm not, at least not any longer. However, my interest in government systems, at the national and sub-national level has been my focus since high school. My parents taught me through their experience to be skeptical of leaders' promises yet hopeful that the right political and social systems would serve the interests of all people. But this is not the reason that I'm writing to you today.

I have returned to Positano several times since I met you. Piero has told me that you were there too, and asked if I wanted to contact you. When we were together we didn't exchange phone numbers and addresses, and I know that I left a day early, probably just hours before we would have shared that information.

When we were together the outside world didn't matter, so phone numbers and addresses didn't matter. Besides, one of my reasons for leaving you so soon was to avoid that moment of truth, the moment when I would be forced to tell you more about myself before I was able to, and that moment when you would ask me for phone numbers and all.

How would I have said no? And, yet, how could I have complied?

I'm sure most of this makes no sense, but it will all come clear.

I'm in Kabul to satisfy some personal needs. It's been a long time coming and it's something that I need to focus on. And you can't be here with me.

It's almost like she was anticipating my questions, and carrying on a dialogue without me in the room.

It won't take me long though, and I expect to return to you and then we'll be together.

Love forever, Gaia.

Gaia's Journal – July 16, 2004, evening

Well, that was sudden. Not the lovemaking – that was slow and lovely.

It was the relationship itself. I've always been a bit reserved, but Danny has swept me off my feet. He's back in his own room, showering for the evening's festivities. What's taking him so long? I thought I was slow!

Just so you know, my little paper conscience, this is a first for me. Well, not men in my life, but love and romance. I'd like to write it off to the atmosphere in Positano – it would make it easier for me to continue with my plan – but it's not just that. It's him.

I have to laugh at that, though. It's not just him; it's me too. I feel different. I even feel like I'm relating to him differently. It's not just that I found someone who fits me perfectly; I've found someone who makes me better, happier, more interesting. And makes me look forward to the future.

As long as I have Danny in it.

We've fallen into a bit of a routine, a lovely routine though. Wake up, dress for the beach, eat a long, leisurely lunch in the shade, wander through the hills that surround Positano, and relax in evenings of fun, music, and exquisite meals. All in the company of wine.

Funny thing, too. As good as the limoncello is here – and it is extraordinarily good – I like sipping glass after glass of local wine with meals or between meals.

Each day is cooled off with chilled glasses of Fiano, and warmed with our own bodies.

This evening will more of the same – Yes! Please! – and I'll have Danny to myself all over again.

This life can't ever end. I have to make sure it doesn't. I wonder if he feels the same way.

May 17, 2007

I lifted the wine-stained glass to my nose again. Thinking that I could still smell the wine, I imagined that we were sitting together on the bed.

I had just drained the contents while Gaia laughed at me with relish. She, too, tipped her glass toward her mouth and, in one draught, emptied it.

Giggling from the effort, a little drop of wine slipped from the corner of her mouth. I caught it with my finger, which she kissed as it lingered on her lips.

We lay back gently onto the cool sheets, my arm draped across her belly, and kissed slowly. But just as I thought we'd stay in that position, she suddenly bolted upright.

"I forgot that I left the iron on in my room!" she said.

Oh, my God, I thought, what terrible timing.

I withdrew my arm and rolled back to let her escape, but she didn't budge. As I scrunched up my brow and made the common palms-up Italian gesture of "what gives?" she laughed and pulled me down upon her.

"Just kidding," Gaia whispered in my ear.

Today, few things make me smile, but that memory did. She liked to tease and, because I was so serious, she often caught me off guard. So, despite my current misery, I smiled. That afternoon, with hunger on my face; today, with resolve and hope.

I reached into the box and withdrew another letter, the next one in the stack. It was dated November 16, 2006. I almost couldn't bear to read it. Whatever it said, by now, I had concluded that it wouldn't be good news.

Gaia wrote it just eight months ago, after more than two years apart. She kept up this correspondence during our absence, although she never shared the letters with me. That is, until she left this box of mysteries with Piero.

Knowing that the letters had covered so many months and that each one revealed more about her to me, and knowing that this recent epistle was drafted not long ago, I moved ahead and opened the envelope.

Gaia's Letter – November 16, 2006

Danny, love, where are you? I need to hold you, and have you hold me. I have been returning to Casa Albertina and Positano and keep hoping to find you there. You'll understand later why I couldn't call you at your work, but I don't know how else to find you.

I'm going to put some papers together, including these letters, and ask Piero to hold them for us. Yes, they're for you and for me.

Do you remember me telling you about my mother and father? They have been so good to me. Theirs was not the easiest life, but they taught me the importance of living according to a set of principles, and staying true to the goals that we set in life.

Some people say my father was a criminal, but he wasn't. Things get all mixed in this crazy world; who gets to say who is a criminal and who is not?

In our time together, I came to know you and to know your heart. You are a good person, Danny, someone that I could love and respect. And the world will love and respect you, but in the end we're just two little people. Two people who have a role to play in the world but who still want to live a life of love together.

I feel like I'm rambling, and maybe I'm not helping much. But I wanted to tell you that I'll find you, or you'll find me. And we'll be together in Positano.

Love you more than life, Gaia.

Mike's Journal – August 1, 2003

Well, Kat was right. We've brought our daughter here to Positano. Serena was born a few years after we got married. She had heard stories of our honeymoon at Casa Albertina and by now (she's eleven years old) she decided she'd like to see it.

This place is just as beautiful and just as magical as I remember it fifteen years ago. Serena stood between Katherine and me on the balcony of the hotel and together we scanned the horizon and took in the gorgeous sunset.

"It's so pretty here," Serena said, a well-thought out understatement by a girl too young yet to fully appreciate that this, the Amalfi Drive, was the prettiest place on earth.

We are staying for a couple of days, just as Kat and I did years ago, and we'll swim in the Mediterranean and eat odd plates of fish, and enjoy many glasses of wine. I'll even let Serena have some; in Europe, the kids are not told to fear wine, they're taught to respect it and enjoy it.

Even today, as I drove our rental car along the tight, narrow, winding ribbon of road that clung to the cliffs of Amalfi, the wondrous scenes spread out below and drew oohs and aahs from both my girls. The tires of the car screeched a bit, but that wasn't because of my speed; I was too nervous to post anything above 25 mph here. Maybe the tires on the car are old, or worn out. And the singing of the rubber on pavement didn't do much to quiet Kat and Serena.

"Mike, you've got to slow down," Kat said.

"If I slow down anymore, the cars behind me will get really mad."

Katherine looked over her shoulder and confirmed that there were three more little Italian autos, all Alpha Romeos probably, and the drivers looked like they were losing their patience with this Americano.

"Okay, but please be careful," she concluded.

I was, and I intended to continue to be, but while Kat and Serena's eyes were glued to the glistening sea below, mine were locked on the twisting white line on the road ahead of me.

We arrived safely – of course – and I parked the car in the space that was allotted for the hotel. Pulling the suitcases out of the trunk we looked up the slope toward the entrance to Casa Albertina. Over the years (and aging) I had forgotten the climb that was involved in reaching our little slice of paradise.

"We're walking up there?" Serena asked, indicating the façade of the hotel with her right index finger.

I nodded, Katherine sighed, and we started out. We had climbed halfway – it seemed like several hundred steps – when Umberto came running down the stairs to our rescue.

"*Buon giorno*," he said greeting us with more energy than I could muster.

"How did you know we were coming?" I asked.

Umberto looked at me, slumped his shoulders, and with loud, heavy breathing mimicked someone climbing steps out of wind. We all got a laugh out of this, Serena especially, but made it the rest of the way without much trouble.

"*Cena é alle otto*," said Umberto, dinner is at eight.

"*Si*," I replied, "*d'accordo*." Agreed. I was enjoying showing off what little Italian I knew for my daughter's appreciation.

"Ask him how to say 'What will the weather be like tomorrow?' " Katherine said.

Serena looked at me expectantly, but I just sneered at Kat for ruining my show. Every dad wants his daughter to be impressed by him, even though we know later in life she'll outgrow the mystique. I just wanted my daughter to stay impressed a little bit longer.

"Actually, Serena," Katherine continued, "your dad's Italian, while not perfect, got us through the airport and train station, and he'll probably also dazzle you tonight at dinner with his selection of dishes."

I could tell Kat was just trying to smooth over her challenge, but I appreciated it.

So, tonight, as we look out on the Mediterranean Sea below, the trees, greenery, and lemon trees that cluster along the slopes above and below, and the crimson glow of the sun as it hugs the watery horizon, I am at peace. My wife and daughter are with me in this glorious place, and nothing could be better.

I am maybe the happiest man alive. Positano has that effect on you I guess.

My Journal – July 17, 2004, morning

Nothing could replace this feeling. We had a fantastic evening and night, filled with food, wine, and love. While I'm no longer sure of the order of importance, the food and wine surely add to the all-consuming pleasure of the day.

I'm sitting up in bed again, in Gaia's room, while she showers. I'd rather be in there with her but she says she needs to be serious about getting ready in the morning.

"Afternoon showers are different," she reminded me with an impish smile.

So I fill the slowly passing minutes with my journal. Oh, sis, if you had only known what these pages would record!

I know what I think of Gaia – she's like the future of my life in a snapshot – but I don't really know what she thinks of me. Well, I think I do. She certainly is interested enough that she'll share her bed with me. And we've spent every available minute together now for the last two and half days. Wow, I sound like a kid, counting the days in fractions.

And Gaia has said some very encouraging things – "Let's not get ahead of ourselves; I want this to last" – is my favorite.

She's certainly a woman that I could build my world around. She's a student of history, so we clearly have that in common. [NOTE to self: Ask her how she got the name Gaia. Greek parents?] So, wherever she's from, I'll have to find out.

Funny thing, I still don't even know what school she goes to.

Last night at dinner, when that came up, I asked her point blank. I wanted to get the geography right, so I could zero in on whether we would have a long- or short-distance relationship. But when I asked, she turned it around.

"You work for State, right? In Washington?"

"Well, no, right now I'm stationed in Afghanistan." The mention of the word was like drawing a dark cloud over our time together. I shook my head to dispel it.

"But you'll be returning to Washington?"

"Yeah, probably, when I'm done here."

"Huh," she uttered with a slight shrug. "Well, that'll be long distance." I couldn't tell whether she meant from Afghanistan, or New York, or wherever she lived.

Before I could force the question, she reached across the table and stroked the back of my hand with her fingers. It so distracted me that I decided to abandon questions for now and just enjoy the moment.

I hear Gaia in the bathroom now. She's out of the shower – my mind conjures devilish thoughts about her state of dress – but then I hear the hair dryer going. She's humming something. I don't recognize it.

If I had to change anything about last night, I would wish we had ordered less food. That sounds strange in Italy, the land of plenty, but as much as we enjoy it all, the bounty seems to put us both in mind of sleep. Not that the bed is an unwelcome place...

Yeah, I suppose the wine plays a part in that also. I asked Gaia if she has converted from limoncello to wine.

"I had heard that the Sorrento lemons make the best limoncello, so I decided to test the thesis," she replied, in almost a professorial tone – "test the thesis."

"But the wine is also so good…the Fiano, Greco, Solopaca…" Gaia had tasted so many she was on a first name basis with the region's great white wines. She didn't call them Fiano di Avellino and Greco di Tufo, just Fiano and Greco, as if these were new friends that she planned to invite to her next party.

"I think, maybe, the wine is easier to sit with and sip over a period of hours. As good as the limoncello is, it doesn't go with a meal."

My preferences always went toward red, like the Falerno and Taurasi that I'd been drinking, but I had to agree that the crisp white wines of Campania were the best option in the heat of the summer sun.

Okay, so now the hair dryer is off and she's still humming.

"What are you doing in there?" I asked.

"Making sure I look as good as you remember," she replied.

Okay, no problem there.

"Just come back to bed," I suggested. That got a reaction.

She stuck her head out the door and gave me a withering look.

"You promised we'd go to Ravello today. Are you reneging on that?"

"No, of course not, I just thought…"

She wouldn't let me get out of that. I had to agree once I got Gaia's naked body out of my mind, that I was looking forward to seeing the hilltop town I had heard so much about.

Once more, Gaia stuck her head out of the bathroom door.

"What are you writing?"

"Oh, nothing," I said as I quickly closed the journal.

I hadn't told her that I was taking notes, and even though the contents of my journal couldn't be more intimate than the moments Gaia and I had spent together, my thoughts inscribed therein were too personal to reveal. I knew then that I had made a mistake retrieving the journal from my room so I could spend more time in her presence. So I called out that I was going back to my room to shower and dress.

"It's about time you got going," she said, teasing evident in her voice.

Gaia's Journal – July 17, 2004, morning

Danny has returned to his room to shower and get dressed. We're going to Ravello today, a place that I read about before coming to Positano. It's an ancient village even higher up on the slopes of the Amalfi Coast than we are right now.

I had fully intended to get there before now (I don't know how; I don't have a car!) but Danny's been occupying a lot of my time. Haha, that's not a complaint! I love it! (I've been using that word "love" a lot lately.)

So, here I am with you, my little journal. What do you want to know?

That I'm happy, that I'm in love, that everything in the world suddenly seems so right and beautiful?

Well, all that's true. And it's thanks to Danny. Our last few days have a been a whirlwind of eating, drinking, and making love. I'm a very serious person, well maybe too serious, and I don't often let myself relax like I have here.

Positano is a terrific place where the activities are all focused on living well. That's not a complaint.

What I mean is there are no libraries, no work to be done, no industry and certainly no government. (Italians would most likely say they have no government anywhere in the country.) There are shops, restaurants, and bars, and I suppose there are more convenience-type stores for the locals, but in the last three days I have had no inclination to think of, or do, anything of substance.

Oops, sorry Danny (that's alright, you'll never read this diary). I didn't mean that our relationship is not something of substance. But if anyone ever wanted to go on a vacation where every day felt truly like a vacation, this is the place!

The sun, the breeze, the smell of the sea, the sound of the waves lapping up the shore. They all combine to make a perfectly lazy day seem like the best moments of your life. I've been to other beaches and have enjoyed swimming in everything from the Atlantic to the Pacific to the Dead Sea and now the Mediterranean. But no beach town has ever left me feeling so completely satisfied as I do now.

Okay, thanks again to you, Danny!

Anyway, I'll write more about Ravello when we have returned from our day trip. That is if I have any time of privacy to write. These little entries are important, but so is time with Danny.

Note to self: I've really got to tell him what I'm doing here.

May 17, 2007

I threw the letter on the bed and walked out to the terrazza. I couldn't take any more of this. I needed a drink and figured I'd get something from Piero or Umberto, whoever was tending the desk.

Well, there was no one tending the desk. I looked around, left and right, and heard a roar of cheering from the back room. Heading in that direction, I saw the cook and waiters clustered around a table staring intently at the television. A soccer game was on and their attention was riveted to the screen.

Umberto came up from behind.

"Signor Danny. Can I help you?"

Another roar from the back room. The local team must have scored.

"Sì, Umberto. Can I get a bottle of wine?"

"Aglianico, *corretto*?"

"*Sì*. Aglianico would be perfect."

Umberto disappeared into the back room and returned with a bottle, a glass, and corkscrew in his hand. Moans and hissing exploded from the back room, accompanied by colorful words of damnation for the blind officials on the soccer pitch.

Setting the bottle down on the desk, Umberto inserted the corkscrew with practiced ease and lifted the cork from the neck of the bottle. He turned the stemless tumbler upside down and nestled it down on the bottle's open top, and handed the ensemble to me.

"*Grazie*," I said, and returned to my room.

Once I had closed the door behind me, I stepped over to the open doorway and stone railing that surrounded my private balcony. I poured a full glass of the wine, sipped once, and then drained the glass. It felt good going down and immediately took effect. It wasn't a soporific effect on my body, but gulping down the contents of the glass helped rest my mind. The alcoholic effect would come soon enough.

I rested my hands on the rounded rail and leaned over slightly to the valley and beachscape below. The fishing boats bobbed in the surf along with the bobbing heads of fathers and children playing in the water. It was the middle of the afternoon, so the sun was still high overhead, and it cast its warm rays on my face.

A breeze blew down from over the hill behind me and whistled through the branches of trees hanging by their roots to this vertical slope. The brilliant colors of green and yellow that marked the dome of the Positano cathedral reflected in the sunlight and danced in the interstices between passing clouds.

Looking left I could see the whole of Positano. It remained as magical to me now as it was three years ago, although the absence of Gaia transformed my impression in ways that I cannot describe.

A knock on my door drew my attention, so I retreated into the room to answer the call. The maid was standing there with fresh towels, but she also bore a tray of food. There was a basket of the local bread, several hunks of cheese, a bowl of olives, and a small plate of fresh figs.

"Signor Piero thanks you for coming to Casa Albertina," she said in memorized English.

I brought the tray out onto the terrace and set it on the table next to the bottle of wine. Choosing what was most needed first, I reached for the bottle, poured another glassful, then lifted it to my mouth. This time, I was a bit more patient, letting the wine slip slowly past my tongue and down my throat, rather than guzzling it like the last time.

Aglianico was then, and is now, my favorite red wine. It's natural flavors and subtle accents remind me of all that is good and great about wine. It's not a cerebral drink, but neither is it a peasant beverage. It goes by many names, including Aglianico del Vulture and Aglianico del Vesuvio, both referring to places in this region. The bottle that I had on the table at that moment had no such special distinguishing characteristic.

And this, perhaps, was the reason it tasted so good. I needed some wine, something to soothe my soul. And Aglianico did just that. I already knew that this bottle would not need recorking tonight.

After sampling a bit of the edibles delivered by the maid, I returned to the box Gaia had left me. There was one letter left in there, dated February 12, 2007. I fanned it back and forth in my hand, deliberating not whether to open it, but rather in how to deal with the contents. It was the latest of her epistles and I, not knowing when the next one would be added by her – or how, now that I had the box – wondered how much information it would contain.

There could be two reasons that this was the sole remaining letter. Either Gaia was telling me in it that this would be the last and then, maybe, she would tell me everything so that I didn't have to wonder anymore.

Or this was not the last letter, only the most recent. It had been written only a few months earlier and there were often months between the dates of her letters. I hope that this was just the latest in a still-incomplete series of messages.

Gaia's Letter – February 12, 2007

Dear Danny,

I can tell you more now, as time gets closer, because I don't want you to worry. Everything will be alright.

I'm writing this letter from a table in Da Vincenzo, the little restaurant we ate at on July 15, 2014. I'm even sitting at the same table, and I think the owner even recognizes me. Funny, that.

Our dinner there was so wonderful, as was the night. I will never forget it. It was fun and exciting, certainly, but that evening with you and the other hours we spent together made me a complete person. I never believed that a woman needed a man to be complete and I still don't – any more than a man needs a woman to be complete – but I do believe that loving someone and being loved back can bring about the most amazing transformation in a person's life. Women love women and are completely happy and fulfilled. Men probably share similar experiences, but for me - - it's you.

I also remember how you drank too much wine that night. Were you nervous around me? I can't believe that's the reason. Maybe we were both just intoxicated with wine, or whatever.

But I promised more detail. Here you go. I have only a little time, but I think I can complete the story. If not, I will finish it in person. That would be good, huh?

I shuddered at this last comment. This is everything that I have wanted. Was she promising to come back? If so, when? I didn't care about her story. I wanted to hold her in my arms.

My father is – was – Ibrahim al Kaatani. He was Sufi, and not well liked by some of those who professed other beliefs from their Muslim faith. My mother is Damiana Panos, a Greek citizen.

They met and married many years ago when the Arab Peninsula was less troubled than it is today. I know, there've been wars in the Middle East for a thousand years, but there were also long periods of relative peace. At least the kind of peace that allowed people to travel in and out of the region, and to meet and fall in love.

In my case, it was my mother who traveled to Kabul and met my father. A new war broke out just after they married and my mother insisted on returning to Greece where they would be safe. My father dawdled and delayed; he didn't want to leave the land of his birth. During that time, I was born.

They named me Gaia Kostopolous. Why not Panos, or al Kaatani? Like I said, these were difficult times and my mother was constantly afraid that I, or she, or all of us would perish. My father was becoming more rebellious and Mama was certain that he would have trouble.

They fought often. I remember that growing up. Not without love. No, they were very much in love, but my mother wanted to leave, needed to leave, and my father refused to.

I grew up there, in a land where wars are fought almost continuously, and where cities are levelled by violence more often than yours are levelled by hurricanes in the States. I wish that the destruction of my cities was from hurricanes. In Afghanistan, you can't blame God or nature so you can accept your fate.

Living and dying by some madman's whim is so much worse.

Her mention of Afghanistan gave me chills. That's where I'm stationed! How could we be in the same country and not find each other? And I had mentioned being stationed in Kabul but Gaia obviously didn't take advantage of that to search me out.

What my mother most feared happened one day. My father, always the rebel, was gunned down in the street by Abdul Amir al Ramadi. I was only ten years old.

It was then that Mama explained to me why they had given me the last name of Kostopolous. She wanted to disguise my connection to my father, to protect me. As a young girl, and with a different name, now living in a different country, she felt that I was safe. Or she thought that, once time had passed, the connection between me and my beloved father would be lost.

Al Ramadi was a ruthless man. He thought of himself as a leader of the Islamic movement, in an endless struggle against Western imperialism. In fact, he was just a minor player for a long time, a self-proclaimed war lord with a minimal following. What he lacked in support and recognition he made up for in brutal treatment of his enemies, or those he perceived as enemies.

My father had argued with al Ramadi in the past. They occupied the same circle of Islam in Kabul, although they didn't agree on their interpretation of its teachings. My father was not against the West, at least not against the society and its institutions. My father wanted the West, particularly the U.S., to show more respect for the traditions of Sufism and broader Islam; al Ramadi wanted the West to go up in flames.

The arguments between the two men escalated progressively over the years until al Ramadi decided to close the argument in the only way his small mind could imagine. Surrounded by several of his supporters, al Ramadi approached my father in the street. My father was unarmed and unprotected; he wasn't looking for trouble. But he must have known what was in store when he encountered al Ramadi armed and standing at the center of other armed men.

Al Ramadi apparently shouted something to my father; the words have never been recounted to me accurately. My father resisted, argued, and turned to go. Al Ramadi lifted his rifle, pointed at the center of my father's back, and released a torrent of bullets that tore through my father's body. He crumpled to the ground as blood spurted and poured from dozens of entry wounds.

I was standing nearby and witnessed it all.

When my father fell, his head hit the ground with his face turned in my direction. In the last reflex of the life that was slipping away from him, my father blinked his eyes once at me. That was his final sign of love. That was his final moment on this earth.

My Journal – July 17, 2004, evening

After breakfast, Gaia and I walked the short distance to the rental car that I had stashed in the hotel parking space. I got in and pulled my seatbelt into place then looked over at Gaia.

"You'd better buckle up yourself," I told her. "I'll drive carefully, but we can't be sure this tiny road won't have surprises coming at us from every bend."

Smiling back at me, she did as suggested.

The road to Ravello stretched across the rocky cliffs and seaside east from Positano, featuring many of the same edge-hugging lanes that I had managed on my drive from Sorrento to the hotel a few days before. At one point, we began to climb the mountain on a brief but scenic drive up to the center of Ravello.

The ancient town itself was high up in the mountain with a clear and infinite view of the Mediterranean which sprawled out in the distance below. We parked the car in a convenient spot in the middle of the town, then hiked to the edge for the view.

A stunning vista – perhaps even better than that from Positano – awaited us. The town itself is quite large, stretching through roadways and piazzas from east to west, but we were in the center of town, near the Duomo Ravello and the Piazza Centrale. This is the center of life in Ravello, and the crystal blue sky and bright sun lit up the stone buildings and colored umbrellas at the cafés that surrounded us.

We spent a lazy afternoon sightseeing around the town, wandering over cobble-stoned streets and under Roman arches that seemed to both pull the buildings together and keep them at arm's length. The Duomo Ravello, the central church in the town, is a fairly simple affair, with whitewashed exterior and unassuming entrance. But the mosaics in the interior are amazing, superbly executed in past centuries.

Gaia pointed to Il Ducato di Ravello on the map, then scanned our surroundings to find it.

"Maybe ducato means duke. This could be the old monarch's residence."

When we found it, we both laughed that it was actually a hotel, not a regal residence. Gaia wouldn't give up though.

"A lot of former royal houses are converted to hotels. This is probably one," she concluded in defense of her argument.

When I googled it on my phone and showed her that it was just a hotel, a very pretty one at that, she shrugged, gave me her most lovely smile, and changed the subject.

We worked up an appetite and stopped at Giardini Caffé Calce which looked good from the outside and whose aromas poured from the open doorway into the street. Our hunger was rewarded with great platters of pasta, exquisitely sweet prosciutto, and grilled asparagus that we both swore we would never forget.

After a long day of walking, we worked our way to the rental car, and noticed a large theatre and bandstand on the edge of town, overlooking the Mediterranean Sea far below. When we asked about it, we were told that this was the time of the Wagner Festival, an annual event in Ravello to commemorate one of the many great musicians and artists who found the town irresistible.

"You are staying for the concert tonight, yes?" we were asked.

Sadly, we weren't, although Gaia made a pitch for extending our stay for a few hours. Deliberating our many options, we decided that our legs and feet needed some rest, and chose to return to Casa Albertina.

Gaia's Journal – July 17, 2004, evening

I just got out of the shower and decided to let my hair air dry. Blow drying works better, but that wild almost animal-like appearance of some of these Italian women convinced me to try the more natural appearance. Let's see if it works.

Danny is in his room showering, so I get to spend a bit of alone time with you. We went to Ravello today. What an amazing place! The views from that high above the Mediterranean, the cute little avenues, and the brightly colored café tables and chairs. I could have – we could have – spent an entire lifetime there.

In fact, we found out that there's a music festival there throughout the summer. Some call it the Ravello Festa, others call it the Wagner Festival. It sounded great, and we wanted to stay, but we had both worn out our feet (and shoes!) and needed to get back to Positano for a siesta.

With Danny!

Besides, I have some planning to do and I can't talk to him about that yet.

Gaia's Letter – February 12, 2007, continued

Mama rushed into the street and saw my father lying prostrate on the rubble. I was still standing in the shadows, a position that she had taught me to take in this war-torn city, and she swept me up and ran back inside.

Once out of harm's way, my mother knelt down in front of me and looked directly into my eyes. Hers were filled with tears; mine were dry and I was in shock. Mama told me about my father's struggle for peace and acceptance, how he had courageously stood up to those who wanted war instead of peace, and how he had preached that Western ways should be left to Western people, just as Eastern people should be allowed to practice Eastern ways.

She wiped the tears from her face with a swipe of her arm, then continued.

"Your father, Ibrahim al Kaatani, was a good man. He was born in the right place but at the wrong time. I would not have had a brilliant husband like him, and you would not have had a loving and devoted father, if he had been born in the time that matched his spirit.

"From this day forward, you will only be known as Gaia Kostopolous. You will not refer to your father and you will not refer to me."

She was confusing me. Even at my young age, I knew that war had been nearly constant and feuds between the tribes unending. Separating me from my father, whose teachings Mama was telling were the thing that had inspired his execution, made some sense, but why did I have to renounce my mother too?

"I'm sending you to my sister's home in Athens," she said. "Al Ramadi knows who I am but he barely knows who you are. He will not let me travel; his men will make sure of that. But if I tried to go with you, he would find you too.

"You must go, before he finds out who you are. You will be safe in Athens. My sister will take care of you, and I will come for you in a while, after al Ramadi forgets about you and looks the other way. Then I will try to find a way to slip out of Kabul and be with you."

Mama looked at me earnestly, peering into my eyes as if to receive a kind of confirmation from me that I understood and that I would comply. Her eyes were filled to the edge, brimming with tears that seem as resolute as she was in not falling.

I never saw my mother again after that day. She didn't come to Athens to collect me and I never heard anything about her destiny. I doubt that she was able to escape Kabul, or she would have come to be with me.

That afternoon, she put me on a bus, with instructions to the man sitting beside me. He was kind and gentle; it seemed like he knew her and was willing to help Mama spirit me out of the country. The driver settled me in a row near the back of the bus. He spread a blanket over my legs because I was shivering. He couldn't know that it wasn't from the cold, but from the loss I had just endured.

After a long trip that included two buses, two car rides through parched countryside, and a swift boat ride across the blue waters of the eastern Mediterranean, I arrived at the Port of Piraeus, near Athens. The boat pulled alongside the dock and men were yelling at the captain and waving their arms, as if to

direct him to another dock. I was too young to understand what was happening, but it was another event
that seemed threatening. I guess I was still in shock
because their loud shouts and gestures just seemed
like background noise in the haze of feelings that
washed over me.

The boat bumped around a bit and, finally, the captain threw a rope to someone standing on the last
few planks of the dock. He pulled mightily on the
end of it, dragging the rickety craft toward him, then
wrestled the rope into loose knots around a wooden
post. The captain stationed himself on the bow of the
boat, and lifted people up to the man on the dock. I
was the last to leave and by then the boat, freed from
the ballast of its passengers, was rocking violently in
the waves cast by passing ships. To finish the effort,
the captain nearly threw me into the arms of the man
on the dock. But I landed safely.

There was a young woman waiting farther down
on the dock, close to shore and squeezed in among
many other bystanders. I didn't know her, and had
never met my aunt if that's who she was. But when
she lifted her face up to me I could see that she bore a

strong family resemblance. I walked down the rough planks of the dock and directly toward her.

"Gaia," she asked. It wasn't a question; it was a statement. She knew I was coming and even what boat I would arrive on, and she was there to collect me.

I nodded yes, and she wrapped me in her arms for a quick hug before leading me away.

On that day, I became Gaia Kostopolous, from Athens, and I tried to erase memories of my earlier life, as my mother had instructed me to do. But Ibrahim al Kaatani and Damiana Panos were still my parents, and with all the love my aunt could provide, I could never erase that.

Mike's Journal – August 2, 2003

Serena is young enough to want to play in the waves but old enough to understand the almost unnatural beauty of this place. She seems especially impressed with all the colors that make up the background of this world. The yellow lemons, the brilliant green shrubbery and potted plants, the deep blue of the sea and the brilliant blue of the sky.

"It's like a painting, Daddy," she said this morning.

We spent our afternoon on the beach, most of it just lying in the sun and soaking up the rays. Languishing on the shoe may have been a bit too lazy for her, so she lured me back into the water. Kat held firm, her fixed smile communicating that, while she liked the water, splashing around in the Mediterranean was not worth messing up her hair.

So Serena and I dove in. There were pockets of people, small kids and families, frolicking in the modest surf of Positano. We dove and lurched about in the water. For a while, I tried lifting Serena up and tossing her back into the water, but at eleven years old and tall for her age, that trick was not as easy as it once had been.

A fishing boat sailed lazily by. It was late in the day for the men to be out, but this one was returning from the day's labors. And it appeared to have been a successful day. One man piloted the craft while another sorted through the largesse of sea creatures on the deck, and a third arranged the nets they had collected to fold and store them in the stern of the boat.

The sun was overhead but this August day was not as hot as I had expected. During Ferragosto, the Italian reference for a nearly universal holiday in August of each year, most urban Italians take time off from work, sometimes for the entire month, and spend it in seaside villages like this one. This is customary because it's so hot in the cities in August that escape is nurturing. But this day in particular was quite pleasant.

I was warned that travel to Italy in August might leave fewer options for us – some museums, many shops, even some restaurants are closed for the month – but family scheduling requirements demanded it. Besides, Positano was open and we would enjoy what we could in Rome, Florence, and Siena while visiting. Squeezing this trip in among work schedules and whatever else was worth it to me; returning to the place Katherine and I had honeymooned – and finally bringing our daughter to see it – was also worth it.

I thought about these things as I watched Serena bobbing and diving through the waves, coming up wet-haired and smiling each time. And I breathed a satisfied sigh as I thought about how important Positano had been to my memory and to my life.

Everything seemed to be made for life's pleasure here, and everything seemed so right. Recalling hectic days at work – not a pleasant thought, though – I was reminded of the importance of Positano in my overall assessment of life. There were challenges aplenty at home, paying a mortgage, raising a child, saving for college – not to mention the more humdrum things like fixing a water pipe or furnace, painting a room in the house, or changing a flat tire on my aging car.

All these seemed like trivia while we were in Positano. Not only were life's little trials more distant, they seemed less important, as if the only things that mattered were the things that we engaged in here, on the Amalfi Coast, in the shadow of Positano.

Right now, we're packing to leave. We'll drive back to Sorrento, spend the night, then take a train to Rome and fly home. The magic of Positano will remain here, but we'll also take some of it with us.

Gaia's Letter – February 12, 2007, continued

Danny, my love, we will be together, but I have to finish something first. Where I have to go, you can't go. What I have to do, you can't help with.

Gaia was not usually this serious – or was she? I suddenly began to wonder how much about her I didn't know. What I treasured about Positano is that it seemed like perpetual vacation, and maybe that was my mistake. Real life existed outside of its hills and beaches, and Gaia's letter was beginning to bring that reality to the fore.

I don't want to think about my duties, or all this time we've spent away from each other, but only to tell you how much you mean to me. I was not expecting to fall in love in Positano. I was taking some time to myself during an important change of life direction, trying to shed old things and prepare myself for new things. I thought I had my future figured out, and then I met you.

I was leaving my carefree days as a student behind; I think by now that you doubted me when I said I was a student. I love history and have been very interested in Middle Eastern politics since I was ten years old, when I faced some ugly truths about the culture I was living in.

My years were spent wondering about how religion can corrupt government, and vice versa, contemplating the Western model and Middle Eastern model, and wondering which parts of each had it right.

I spent several years at university analyzing not only the historical precedents, but also my own feelings about the differences. And how these differences impacted my life. I decided that the Western model of separating religion from government was smarter, and probably created a more balanced culture. The model we see in the Middle East marries the two, which makes it harder for either the religious rules or the government agencies to adjust to slow evolution of the culture which supports them. But I lived in both, the Middle Eastern model in my first ten years and the Western model while a student in America and living in Greece.

I mourned for my father – and I wondered ceaselessly what had happened to my mother. In a way, they had both given up their lives for me – my father in teaching me the fair and tolerant way of living, and my mother in getting me out of Kabul before I was swept into the tides of violence.

In the twelve years since I last saw my mother, I have had to face the reality that she was probably killed by al Ramadi too. And likely thrown into a mass grave. This last chapter in her life and the possibility that she rests with the broken bones of unnamed others may have been known to my aunt, but too disturbing to convey to me.

For years, I didn't know what I was going to do. I love you but I hate al Ramadi and I've been torn between two worlds. Love and hate. Isn't there some line in Shakespeare that will explain all this to me?

Tell me, my darling, you're always so good at quotes. Tell me what some great philosopher would say about my dilemma and lead me to the right path.

My Journal – July 17, 2004, late evening

I feel like I've spent my whole life with Gaia. Yet I can't picture her – or me – in any place other than Positano.

This has been remarkable, and it seems to become more remarkable with each passing hour.

Three days ago we hadn't met. Then, as if a comet had streaked across my horizon, I discovered her on the edge of my world. A light conversation (admittedly filled with great trepidation on my part) led to laughter and love, and a growing attachment I now realize that I cannot afford to lose. And I will do anything in my power to make sure I don't.

I have come to the conclusion that Gaia feels the same way. No proof yet – she might just be enjoying a little Roman holiday with me playing Gregory Peck (okay, Gaia as Audrey Hepburn – I can handle that!). But our time together is too hot, our words too soft, for me not to believe that this is something special.

In any case, Gaia, if you ever read this, here is my declaration: I love you as I have loved no other woman. If you leave me, it'll break my heart. If you swear to stay with me, you will make me the happiest man on earth.

Okay, I've said it. (Of course, I realize that you're not actually going to read this, but it felt good to write it down.)

Gaia's Letter – February 12, 2007, continued

Gaia Kostopolous is my real name, but before we met I made a decision about the direction my life would take, a direction that I cannot change. Some things you can't un-volunteer for.

My other name is Karimi Istafan, and I work for your country, for the CIA.

Over the years since he killed my father, Abdul Amir al Ramadi has grown more violent and has relentlessly pursued a personal vendetta against all Americans, no matter their age or gender, their guilt or innocence. He has killed children, unarmed women, and crippled old men while terrorizing the province and demanding that all the people there support his campaign of murder against Americans.

His followers have grown, and many innocent people have been slain by his sword just because they choose to lead lives of solitary peace. Al Ramadi does not accept peace. He has said at times that he hopes to die in the act of killing his enemy.

The CIA contacted me. Their intelligence is better than his and they knew that I was the daughter of Ibrahim al Kaatani, one of al Ramadi's many victims. I hate al Ramadi and want to see him dead, but I had formulated no concrete ideas of getting revenge; I just hoped for that reality to come true.

The contact by the CIA changed all that.

At first, the agent met with me in Athens just to talk. He approached me in a small Greek restaurant when I was alone. It was on Areos, near Katsatsidis Paulos and Hadrian's library.

"I'm very sorry that your father was killed. And, it seems, in cold blood," he said. He was compassionate, at times shaking his head in disbelief at the blood-shed that stained my homeland.

"We know that your father was a good man, and that al Ramadi executed him simply because their beliefs differed."

The agent was good. He used all the right words. "Good" and "killed in cold blood" to refer to my father; "executed" to refer to al Ramadi's act.

Long into the conversation, he switched subjects.

"Apparently," the agent said, "killing your father wasn't enough. You lost your mother, too."

My head began to spin. What did he know about my mother? I wanted him to tell me, but he waited, staring at me.

Months later I realized that the agent was working me during that interview. I could recall the conversation perfectly and as I repeat his message again today, I know that he was steering me without making bold claims.

"Al Ramadi has killed many people," he continued. Without stating bluntly that al Ramadi had killed Mama, he led me to believe that she too had been murdered. At that point it didn't matter whether al Ramadi had done it; my blood boiled.

I was twenty-two years old at that time. My innocence was claimed back when I was just ten, but it took more years to completely destroy the hopes and rosy illusions of a young girl snatched from a war zone. Even coddled in the peace and safety of Athens, my skin burned when I thought about the rape and ravaging of my homeland, all done in the name of Allah. Al Ramadi and others like him were destroying my country.

"What do you want me to do?" I asked the CIA agent.

May 17, 2007

My hands shook as I read Gaia's words and as I delved deep into the person whose soul I thought I already knew. She was a child of war, forever scarred by public killings – worst of all seeing her own father gunned down before her eyes. She was an orphan of war, ripped from her parents in an effort to save her from the same fate; vainly trying also to wipe away the memories of the atrocities she had lived to see.

Gaia, or was it Karimi, was a young woman with bloodshed and murder laced into her very being; a woman who could rise above the wreckage of her society but who could never put the parts of the culture she loved back together again.

And yet Gaia was also a warm, loving woman whose smile could light up the room and whose love could rescue my lonely heart. She could bring me, a man whose childhood was one of safety and security in America, back from my temporary experience with war in Afghanistan, and return me mentally and emotionally to the safe, secure world that I had known as a youngster.

My early life was free of threats and war, while my adulthood was immersed in it. Gaia's experience was exactly the opposite. She grew up in war but matured in peace.

Are we all inevitably dragged back to the experience of our childhood? Are our experiences as adults simply a shimmering veneer on the more personal, permanent experiences that are etched in our youth?

My eyes filled with tears and I lifted the letter back up to read again. I had to dry my eyes first with the corner of the bedsheet, but proceeded to read Gaia's letter once more.

Gaia's Letter – February 12, 2007, continued

The agent leaned forward on the table, propping his elbows on it and speaking softly to me then.

"We don't want you to get messed up in this war, Gaia. We only want to catch Abdul Amir al Ramadi and stop him from destroying your town and killing the people in it."

"That's what I want," I replied. I was being guided down a path, and the agent was essentially programming what my responses would be. He was good at what he did.

"We know that, at birth, your parents gave you the name of Gaia Kostopolous because they feared al Ramadi would connect you with your father, and find you. We've checked into this very carefully. We would like you to assume another identity, that of Karimi Istafan, and return to Kabul. We are confident that assuming this identity would not raise any suspicion by al Ramadi or his followers.

"You have not been to Kabul for over ten years, right?"

I nodded. It had been just nearly twelve. He already knew the answer to his question.

"So, al Ramadi won't recognize you by your looks either."

I only nodded; we both knew the answer.

The agent told me they hoped I would help with what they were doing.

"What is that, exactly?" I asked him. I needed more details. I was getting uncomfortable and wanted to know what their plan was, what my help would actually be, what danger I would be in.

We talked for a long time. I got another cup of coffee but he just sat there, smoking little Greek cigarettes.

He said he wanted me to work my way into al Ramadi's inner circle. I knew that was crazy, and very dangerous, and I told him so.

"Yes, I understand, this would be very risky for anyone from your family."

Saying my "family," instead of just saying it would be risky for me, he brought images of my father and mother back to me. By saying "family" he reminded me of the broader circle of this battle. He reminded me of what I had lost, not just what I would be risking.

"But some things are also necessary if we are to end this evil reign." The agent looked intently at me with this comment, enlisting me without waiting for a positive reply.

We finished our discussion soon after that, and I said I would have to think about it.

"Yes, of course. I understand."

He stood up and straightened his back, looming over at the table. I stood too, shook his hand and said "I'll get back to you," although I had concluded in that brief few seconds that I would accept the risk. The agent had guided me carefully and very effectively.

By the time we walked out of the café, the feeling of revenge had already possessed me.

My Journal – July 18, 2004

I'm sitting on the edge of my bed, in my room, completely confused about today and what to do with the rest of my life.

This morning I woke up in Gaia's bed – the smell of her hair is still in my mind. I kissed her forehead and, while she rose to shower, I put on my clothes to return to my own room and shower.

I was humming the tune that Gaia had hummed so often, and I was smiling as I thought of her. I toweled off, set the razor and shaving cream out, and went about my usual routine of getting ready for the day. Within ten minutes, I walked out of the bathroom and retrieved some clothes for the day. We had decided to take a long walk around the ridge of Positano, so I chose a short sleeve shirt but long pants, in case we wandered off the path and into the trees.

I brushed my hair, checked my appearance in the mirror, smiled, then stepped out into the hallway.

When I got to Gaia's room I didn't knock. She would have left the door unlocked and so I just pushed it open and stepped into the room.

I expected to see her done with her shower, dressed, and ready to go. By then the sun shone brightly through the open shutters while a wisp of cool morning air slipped between the barely open French doors leading out to her balcony.

But she wasn't in bed, so I went to find her in the shower. With no sound of water running, I thought she might be tending to more private business, so instead of pushing the door open and embarrassing her, I listened carefully for any sounds. Hearing none, I knocked. Getting no response, I turned the doorknob and let myself in.

The bathroom was a bit rumpled as always – Gaia's surroundings always seemed to reflect the casual relationship she had with life – but there was no sign of her. A towel was on the floor and a spent makeup bottle on the sink, which was when I noticed it.

The door to the cabinet next to the sink was ajar. Pulling it open with my fingers, I saw that it was empty except for the various toiletries that were put in the room by the maid. There was nothing that I would identify with Gaia. I hadn't checked her inventory of personal effects, so I didn't know what I would find, but there were clearly no items that belonged to her alone.

I spun on my heels and went through the door into the bedroom area. A sudden breeze blew the door open and whipped around my head, then died down. I pulled the door to the armoire open and saw nothing. No clothes, no suitcase; only empty hangers scattered carelessly across the hanging bar and the floor.

My first reaction was that I was in some sort of time warp. I even wondered momentarily if I had imagined it all, but that wasn't possible. Gaia's body, the scent of her hair, her smile, her eyes... everything, were too real to me. I could even still call up the feeling of her lips against mine just one hour before.

There was a note propped against the lamp on the nightstand. It said only:

"Danny, I love you but I must leave for now. I hope you understand.

"We will be together again, if you will still have me.

"Love, Gaia"

Gaia's Letter – February 12, 2007, continued

I accepted the agent's mission. There were no papers to sign, no employment application, no background check. He – I should say "they" since the CIA was behind this – already knew everything about me. Plus, confidential informants (I had become a "CI") didn't have to be trusted. They were kept in place, and in play, because it would be even more dangerous to quit.

Before long, I was back in Kabul with instructions to find out more about al Ramadi. I was supposed to do this casually, not to investigate him but to show interest in his work and his plan for Western invaders, as he called them. I was told to be faithful to Islam and to demonstrate at least a modest distrust for Americans. With these traits, I was going to establish myself, this new Karimi Istafan, as a potential recruit in the war against the West.

I followed their instructions very well. I found ways to communicate my progress and any information I uncovered back to my contact. It was not the agent who had signed me up in Athens. When I returned to Kabul, I was given new information and a new person to communicate with. He met me only once when I first returned to the city. He gave me a phone number and a place to hide anything like written material where he could find them. He said he would also leave information in that hiding place; occasionally he left new phone numbers for me to call, to keep changing the contact method.

Twice when I checked our hiding place I found new cell phones, and instructions on how to destroy the phone I was using, including wiping the SIM card and destroying any signs that it had been used by me.

I had to be patient, to establish myself as Karimi in Kabul, and build a life there so that I wouldn't be suspected. After about ten months, I saw al Ramadi in a café. He was surrounded by his men and they were laughing about some villagers from outside the city that they had executed that morning. When I heard their conversation, I recalled seeing bodies hanging from tree limbs, their lower limbs seared and still smoking from the torch that had lit their clothes on fire.

Al Ramadi looked at me as I entered the café. I was wearing a *niqāb*, which covered my face but left my eyes exposed. At first, he looked sternly at me, but he softened while staring at me. I could tell by his upturned lip and leer that he was imagining sexual thoughts.

My skin crawled at the sight of him. The only time I had sexual thoughts was about you, and to have this monster imagine the unimaginable about me brought the color up in my face and made my eyes water.

I worried that this reaction might give me away, but he only laughed. I think he was proud that he could get a reaction out of me.

Two months after that, a man came to my house and told me to come with him. Al Ramadi wanted to see me, he said.

I went with the man, knowing that this was the next step according to the CIA plan.

I hoped that my American contact was watching. I hoped that he was also guarding me in the process.

I walked behind the man in the tradition of women in this society, and we entered a small stone house on the outskirts of the market area. There were children in the street, but they were not playing with the carefree abandon that I remember from my childhood in Athens. Passing through the entrance and then a small anteroom, I saw Abdul Amir al Ramadi sitting on a long, low couch, drinking hot tea and talking to several men.

"You are a devout Muslim, no?" he said.

"Yes, I am," I replied, dutifully bowing my head according to the custom when a woman speaks to a man.

He didn't say anything else to me, but signaled for one of the women to come in. She was dressed in a *burqa*, which hid her entire face so I couldn't tell much about her. She led me into another room. I thought it would be to outfit me in the same way, but she spoke only of reading the Quran. I was still getting used to seeing things through the narrow eye slit of the *niqāb*, but managed.

This was another skill that I had developed since returning to Kabul. Although my parents raised me to respect the cultures of both Islam and Greece, I was slow to learn to read Arabic as a child. When I returned to Kabul on this assignment, the agent told me to be scrupulous about learning this, since a failure to be able to read the holy text would be noticed.

We did that for some time, and I noticed the woman paying close attention to my pronunciation. Afterward, thinking about that afternoon, I realized that this reading exercise was the test that allowed me to pass into al Ramadi's army.

That was it. I was led out of the house through a back door, and told to return to my home and wait. I left a brief written report of the meeting in the CIA agent's hiding place. The very next day he left another new phone and told me to destroy the one I had. I knew that he sensed a new opportunity and he wanted to break any thread that might connect me to him.

He also left me instructions for what to do in finding out about al Ramadi's plans.

But I had a plan of my own.

Gaia's Journal – July 18, 2004, morning

I don't have much time. You're in the shower and I have to act fast.

I wish I could tell you what I'm doing, but that wouldn't be right. It would also terrify you and might make me regret my plans. I can't let that happen.

This is so awful.

May 17, 2007

I have no idea what happened that morning. I spent hours looking for Gaia. Piero didn't see her leave, nor did Umberto. I wasn't gone that long, she couldn't have escaped from Positano that quickly.

I went outside and questioned people passing by.

"Did you see a taxi here in the last few minutes? Did you see a woman with long brown hair go out?"

No one saw her; no one had anything to contribute.

Panicking, I ran back into the hotel and straight to her room. The bedding, bathroom, and accessories were there, just as I had seen them. I didn't know what I expected to find on my return to the room, but I was at a loss.

It was inconceivable in that moment that she could just disappear. What had happened?

Naturally, I immediately blamed myself. First, I blamed myself for saying something stupid, or idiotic, or saying something that was so out of place that I had run her off. Then I blamed myself for not seeing what was probably obvious. That Gaia was never that interested in me and she had to sneak away to avoid admitting this to me.

As I sorted through the various possibilities, I suddenly acknowledged the one thing that never seemed to apply. Maybe Gaia was already married, off in Positano on a fling, but realizing that she had gotten herself into something a little too deep, simply fled the scene.

None of these passed the test of my questions. Each time I recalled her comments and her looks, each reasoned possibility seemed less likely.

I reread the note:

"Danny, I love you but I must leave for now. I hope you understand.

"We will be together again, if you will still have me.

"Love, Gaia"

When would we be together again? I sank into the pile of sheets on her bed and wept until my chest heaved and my eyes burned.

Gaia's Letter – February 12, 2007, continued

Over time, maybe months, I became a regular member of al Ramadi's inner circle. His army had murdered scores of civilians, Muslims like him and me, and a handful of Americans. He said all Muslims went to heaven and all Americans went to hell, so the exchange of lives was worth it.

The CIA contact wanted me to report all of this and warn the Americans of a possible suicide attack, which I did. But I also was going to follow through on my plan to kill al Ramadi. I knew that his men would never let me get near him with a weapon, but I would have to try.

One day, al Ramadi called me to come closer so that he could speak with me.

"Our women can fight the same battles as the men, you know," he said.

That was a bit strange, because in Islam the men are the fighters. But I also knew that some Muslim women had joined the armed resistance.

"Would you fight the battle with us, Karimi?"

I nodded yes. Al Ramadi smiled warmly then, and called over one of the men to take me away.

Women fought, it's true, but they rarely used rifles against the Americans. Women were drafted to serve as suicide bombers, though.

May 17, 2007

I stared at the letter through my tears, and let it fall to the bed. I sat numb on the edge of the bed. I couldn't believe what I was reading. This seemed to have been written by some woman I'd never met, not Gaia.

She was consorting with a known murderer, and being enlisted to serve as a suicide bomber.

I picked up the letter and resumed reading.

Gaia's Letter – February 12, 2007, continued

I knew that I could never approach al Ramadi with a weapon, and if I failed at this attempt I would be killed instead.

I knew that al Ramadi liked to meet with the suicide bombers alone before they went off on their mission. It was his habit to kneel in prayer with the person, to wish them well on this day and in their afterlife. If I agreed to serve as a bomber, he would bring me into his room and no one would be there except me and al Ramadi. And I would have my chance.

Such an invitation didn't go out until the bomber was fully committed to the act. The vest would be assembled and strapped in place around the person's chest, but the detonator would not be inserted until after the prayer and just as the bomber departed for his mission. I knew all this because I had been studying al Ramadi's behavior and tactics for weeks.

I also knew the man who inserted the detonator, how he did it, and what device he used.

I couldn't tell my CIA contact what I was planning; he would take me out of the city to prevent me from carrying out my own vendetta.

I want you to know how much I love you, Danny. That will never change. And if the heavens will it, I will be back in your arms soon. *Inshallah.*

Love, Gaia

It was impossible for me to read what she was saying. Not only did I not want to face the fact that Gaia was contemplating the risk of carrying an explosive belt around her chest; I also couldn't figure out why she was calling on the heavens to bring us back together again. Had she sealed her fate, or was this another play of disinformation?

That was the end of her letter, the last in the box.

May 18, 2007

I didn't get any sleep last night, and I knew I wouldn't. The story Gaia told in her letters and in her journal left me bereft of hope. My beloved, whom I had pledged my undying love for, had put herself in a dangerous position to carry out an act of revenge.

I can't live without her but after three years of trying I haven't been able to find her. Now, when she leaves me a time capsule of our time together, I feel both closer to and farther from her at the same time.

The sun shines brightly through the doorway into my room as I gather my things to pack. I feel like I've exhausted all my means of finding Gaia, and now I must wait until she finds me.

Rethinking what Piero said yesterday, I had to admit it's true. Gaia wants to find me here, not at the State Department, but I can't move to Positano.

But why not, I started thinking? I was finished with my posting in Afghanistan. Maybe I should quit my job and move here permanently. I could stay here year-round and wait for the moment when Gaia returns.

I finished packing my bags and wheeled them out into the hallway, where Umberto and Piero stood talking. Seeing me, they looked up and, without smiling, awaited my approach.

"You're going back to Afghanistan, Danny," Piero said.

"No, I'm finished there. I'm going to the States. I don't have a specific assignment yet, but it won't be Afghanistan."

"Maybe it will be Positano," Umberto offered lamely.

That drew a wan smile from me.

"Probably not," I responded.

"And what will you do now, Danny?" asked Piero.

I shrugged my shoulders.

"I'll go stateside, wait for an assignment, then begin again."

"And Gaia?" he asked.

It was a brave question. He knew the sound of her name would be painful for me, but Piero knew me well by that time and wanted to find out how I was doing.

"I'll keep looking for her, but probably have to wait for her to contact me. Will you promise to help me in this? If Gaia comes back here, please, please, please make her call me. Or give me an address to work from. Anything."

Piero just nodded his head. There was little he could add.

Mike's Journal – August 3, 2003

It's time to go, but it's hard to convince an eleven year old of the necessity for schedules. Serena insisted on one more splash in the Mediterranean. I'm writing these last notes down before we return to the hotel to retrieve our bags.

She loves the pebbly beach, the bright sun, and blue waters. Kat and I are relaxing on the beach while watching our little one in the water. What a day! What a place!

Gaia's Journal – July 18, 2004, last entry

I have to hurry. I know you'll be coming through the door at any moment and I can't let you find me here. If I see you again in front of me, I'll never be able to follow through with this.

You will understand, Danny. I promise, and I love you.

Mike's Journal – August 3, 2003

Serena now knows what Kat and I fell in love with. Positano is like heaven. It's the place where love and life come first, where Katherine and I sealed our marital pact, where we drew together into a lifelong bond.

That may sound over the top, but sitting here in the lobby of Casa Albertina while the girls finish packing, I'm drawn back to my first days here with Kat in 1988 and to these few days together with her and Serena this summer. It's a magical place.

May 26, 2007 – Washington, D.C.

I've made it back to my old office in Washington, D.C. It's seems so different now, even though I've been here for a week already. I had made occasional visits to the Washington office during my four-year stint in Afghanistan, but now that I'm sitting behind my old desk and sorting through the files, it feels both like I had never left and also like it's not my place anymore.

Gaia still occupies my thoughts. I pressed Piero to keep an eye out for her which, thinking back, sounded stupid. If Gaia comes to Positano, it would be to find me (I hope) and she will certainly go to Casa Albertina. But I couldn't leave the hotel without reminding Piero how much I needed to find her.

"*Sì, sì.* I know, Danny. I will call you as soon as I see her."

"And don't let her leave. Even if you have to hold her against her will."

Like anyone could hold Gaia against her will.

The daily mail arrives and I sort through the contents. This isn't like my mail at home, packed with unsolicited advertisements and promises of quick credit. This mail is nearly all classified communication, with an occasional unclassified but official notice tucked in the pile.

I arrange the parcels in piles. It's a habit I picked up over the years. There is so much to read that I have to sort them into "now," "later," and "maybe" piles. There's also the email to contend with but, even using a classified server, we communicate mostly in paper for this type of information.

Suddenly, I see my name, Danny d'Amato, on a crisp, cream-colored envelope. The "y" has a familiar swirl to it and my heart leaps from my chest. Even with no return address, I know it's from Gaia. She knows where I am, probably always did know, but this is the first time she's tried to reach me anywhere outside of Positano.

It's dated April 12. Barely six weeks ago.

My Journal – May 18, 2007

I am sitting in my room waiting for the taxi to arrive to take me to Sorrento and then on to the airport in Rome. The moments pass by so slowly.

I feel like my life has ended. I have searched for Gaia for three years before finally getting some word from her. But from her journal and letters, I still don't know what to do, where to find her, or even if she wants to be found.

I know that she was in Kabul as of February, just three months ago. It strikes me as painfully sad that I was in the same country as Gaia for so long and didn't know it. That I was looking for her here in Positano, as she was looking for me here, when we occupied the same small space on the globe together for three years.

But she knew that too. She knew I was stationed in Afghanistan, and knew that she was there. Did she ever try to find me while we were together in Kabul?

There was the time when I was driving back into town, muscling the same dusty station truck that we were all assigned. On the side of the road, I saw some

189

boys kicking something around, until I realized that it was the severed head of some animal. They were mimicking the Afghans' sport of *Buzkashi*, where two teams of horsemen fight over the body of a dead goat.

As I passed through crowds on the street, a small bunch of women clothed head to toe stood by the side. Women seldom turned their attention to a man on the street, particularly not an American. But I noticed one woman daring a quick glance in my direction. At the time, it meant nothing to me. Now, knowing that Gaia lived in Kabul during that period, I thought back and wondered whether it was her.

Such things torment a lost soul.

Gaia's Letter – April 12, 2007

My dearest Danny,

I'm so sorry, my love, that I must write you this letter. You already know about my mother and father, and about my being enlisted by the CIA to find out more about Abdul Amir al Ramadi. So, I won't repeat all that here.

But you must know how much I loved my parents, and how al Ramadi killed them. Well, I know he killed my father, gunned him down in cold blood. I fear only the worst has happened to my mother.

My father didn't deserve to die, but he does deserve *qiṣāṣ*.

I knew this word, qiṣāṣ. It's the reference to Sharia law, and to Westerners it means "an eye for an eye." Revenge.

According to Sharia law, *qiṣāṣ* gives me the right, no, the duty, to take al Ramadi's life. I have found a way and I hope you will forgive me for my absence, my failure to contact you directly, and what I am about to do.

I am not a killer, but I must avenge my father's death.

The time we spent together in Positano were the best days of my life. You awakened in me a spirit that I had never imagined. From my earliest childhood spent in war, to the death of my parents, to suddenly being cast out of my home in Kabul, I had known much pain and loss. But you were like a spirit that came to me from above. Your smile and kind words – oh, yes, I laughed hard at your silly comments – these showed me how wonderful a life lived in peace could be.

But I am a child of war, and some experiences can never be washed from the soul. The taint of death and bloodshed is a part of me and with all the good you were for me, I realized when I returned to Kabul that this carnage had forever changed the person I might have been.

I love you, Danny. I will always love you. I hope that you will forgive me. Please, forgive me.

Gaia

June 3, 2007 – Washington, D.C.

My interest in Abdul Amir al Ramadi increased when I returned to my D.C. office. Since finding out that Gaia was in Kabul, and in al Ramadi's circle of fighters, I read everything I could about him. He was still little more than a bit player, but his activities had attracted enough attention from the CIA that they wanted to keep him on their radar screen.

I was even able to bring up video clips of some of his movements. I memorized his face after hours of viewing, sometimes at night when most of the State department was quiet and dark. I studied al Ramadi's various homes, all treated like hideouts. It was commonplace for a man in his position to move about several residences, move his meetings from the city to the countryside, and generally create confusion concerning his whereabouts.

Al Ramadi had little reason to fear being killed; he was too small a player in the war for the CIA to want to neutralize. But his ego was bigger than his reputation, and he mimicked the actions of more formidable terrorists as part of his lifestyle, to convince his retinue that he was more important than he actually was.

And I studied the film for other people who surrounded him. The men were mostly bearded and young; only a few older men were members of al Ramadi's army. There were several women; judging from a collage of the videos I counted maybe seven in all. It was essentially impossible to distinguish the women one from another. In robes and *niqāb*, only their eyes showed through and from the cameras' distant position, no details were available to make one woman stand out over another.

I ran through the videos again, focusing on the ones with women in clusters. I thought that this would give me a chance to compare them according to their body type. Height, overall weight, how they carried their shoulders. When I tried to imagine how they looked under the robes, I recalled Gaia's body, naked next to me, and I shuddered.

She was one of them in this crowd. Based on her letters she was among this throng of people. How could I reach out to her?

I even tried to identify her contact in Kabul, her CIA handler. But the D.C. contact for chief of Kabul station rebuked me. I wasn't cleared for that information and she said she couldn't tell me who was working with this woman, Karimi Istafan. That would violate protocol and, not incidentally, risk her life by exposing her to al Ramadi.

Another stack of mail arrived and, as he was leaving my cubicle, the clerk mentioned that there was some news that I would be interested in.

"You're spending a lot of time on al Ramadi, aren't you?" he asked.

I nodded my head.

"Well, you might want to check the video we uploaded this morning."

I dashed to the screening room and called up the morning's clips. There were dozens of them relating to activities throughout the region, some specific to Kabul, but it took me over an hour to find the video I was looking for.

It started with a still shot of Abdul Amir al Ramadi. A close-up shot taken from an angle above him (obviously a picture taken from a rooftop) but I knew it was him. His medium-length salt and pepper beard, and his long shaggy hair gave him away. Even without that, I would have recognized him from the sword that he always kept strapped to his waist.

The still shot faded and a video started. This one was a bit more distant, probably a drone shot. It showed people milling about in a bombed-out inter-section of Kabul. There was al Ramadi in the middle of the crowd, surrounded by three men and a woman in *niqāb*.

Suddenly, a brilliant flash filled the screen and smoke obscured the picture for a few seconds. When it cleared, there were bodies scattered around the square, and some people who survived the bombing but seriously injured, dragging themselves towards the fringes of the blast zone and away from what had recently exploded.

This video was replaced by a black screen and a narrative:

In the early morning hours of June 3, 2007, in Kabul, a suicide bomber's vest detonated in the vicinity of Abdul Amir al Ramadi. It's likely that the explosion was unintentional, but it killed al Ramadi and three others in his group, including the suicide bomber.

The station chief has confirmed through various sources the death of Abdul Amir al Ramadi. Current identification of the suicide bomber is not yet available; however, but it is believed to be the person shown here.

The picture went black, and then a closeup of a woman dressed in *niqāb* filled the screen. The image could not have been taken surreptitiously; it was too close. Only her eyes were visible through the eye slit of the robes. And they stared back at me.

Her eyes were brown, with little green flecks that sparkled against the background of the iris.

Ten Years Later – Positano

I'm sitting on the beach here in Positano again. So many years have passed and yet I am still drawn inexplicably to this same spot. I didn't check in at Casa Albertina yet; that will come. I needed first to sit on the beach, look at the Mediterranean Sea, and think about Gaia and my life here with her.

Suddenly, Piero appeared at my shoulder.

"Danny! I didn't know you were coming. Will you not be staying at Casa Albertina?"

"Yes, I have a reservation. Didn't Umberto tell you?"

"No," he said with a chuckle. "I'll have to speak to him about that."

We looked at each other for an awkward moment, not knowing what to say next. Piero broke the silence.

"Gaia didn't come back, Danny. I would have told you. You believe me, don't you?"

I nodded, but couldn't bring myself to tell Piero all that I knew about Gaia. She was gone, killed by her own plan, and there was no reason to burden him with this news.

A moment later, my two children ran up from the water's edge, startling Piero.

"What? Who are these beautiful children?" he asked with a broad smile.

"They are mine. They are beautiful, aren't they?"

Piero scrunched up his brow, fumbling for the right words.

"No," I said to take the mystery out of it. "They are not Gaia's children. You would have known that, right, my friend?"

Piero nodded, but he seemed a bit more relaxed, probably sensing that my life had taken a good turn.

"And your wife?" he asked.

I lowered my eyes for a second and studied my hands.

"My marriage didn't work out." It was a difficult admission, but I knew why it had failed. And I think that Piero saw through to the real reason too.

"But I have these wonderful kids who are still mine, and I wanted them to see this beautiful place."

"What are their names?"

"This is Peter. He's four years old."

"Four and a half," my son corrected, and I smiled.

"And this gorgeous little girl is Tara. She's three…and a half," I said, not waiting to be corrected.

Piero smiled and studied the children for a moment, then spoke.

"Tara," he said.

I nodded.

"Tara, or Terra as the English say it, is the Roman goddess of the earth, isn't she?"

I looked down again and nodded my head. Piero and I both knew that Gaia was the Greek goddess of the earth.

"Well, I better be going back to the hotel," Piero said to break the silence.

"Wait," I interjected. Reaching into my rucksack I pulled out my journal, and the one that Gaia had written, and handed them to Piero.

"We didn't leave these journals at the hotel all these years, like so many of your other guests do. But I want you to have them. You can put them in our rooms now, if you want. I won't be reading them anymore."

Piero took the volumes from me and stared at them.

"Okay, Danny, but I'd rather not put them in the two rooms. If you agree, I'd like to put both journals in Gaia's room, together."

I nodded my head in assent.

Just as Piero was turning to walk away, I added one more request.

"Do you have any blank books on hand? I think I'll be starting a new story."

Piero bowed his head and smiled.

"But of course, my old friend. Of course."

Mike's Journal – August 3, 2003

The girls are ready and the suitcases are standing in the lobby.

I'm so glad we came back here, and that Serena finally had a chance to see Positano.

If I ever return to Positano, or if I never return to Positano, I will always remember it. It is the most romantic place on earth.

"So we beat on, boats against the current, borne back ceaselessly into the past."
        - F. Scott Fitzgerald, *The Great Gatsby*

Dear reader,

We hope you enjoyed reading *A Love Lost In Positano*. Please take a moment to leave a review in Amazon, even if it's a short one. Your opinion is important to us.

Discover more books by D.P. Rosano at https://www.nextchapter.pub/authors/author-dp-rosano

Want to know when one of our books is free or discounted for Kindle? Join the newsletter at http://eepurl.com/bqqB3H

Best regards,

D.P. Rosano and the Next Chapter Team

You might also like:

A Death In Tuscany by Dick Rosano

To read first chapter for free, head to:
https://www.nextchapter.pub/books/a-death-in-
tuscany

Printed in Poland
by Amazon Fulfillment
Poland Sp. z o.o., Wrocław